about the author

chad kultgen graduated from the University of Southern California School of Film and Television. He lives in California. This is his first book.

the average american male

the average american male

a novel

chad kultgen

NEW YORK • LONDON • TORONTO • SYDNEY

HARPER PERENNIAL

This novel is a work of fiction. Any references to real people, events, establishments, organizations, or locales are intended only to give the fiction a sense of reality and authenticity and are used fictitiously. All other names, characters, and places and all dialogue and incidents portrayed in this book are the product of the author's imagination and are not to be construed as real.

HarperCollins books may be purchased for educational, business, or sales promotional use. For information please write: Special Markets Department, HarperCollins Publishers, 10 East 53rd Street, New York, NY 10022.

FIRST EDITION

Designed by Joy O'Meara

Library of Congress Cataloging-in-Publication Data is available upon request.

ISBN: 978-0-06-123167-4
ISBN-10: 0-06-123167-3

12 13 ❖/RRD 20 19 18 17 16

the average american male

chapter one

Christmas with Mom and Dad

Same old bullshit.

chapter two

The Flight Back to L.A.

It's two days after Christmas. I'm in Denver International Airport watching this old fat bitch eat a cup of yogurt. My blood is boiling.

She has this weird little baby spoon, and these leathery fucking jowls, and this twitchy mouth, and her little tongue keeps jerking around to lick this shit off her lips—it's really fucking disgusting me. But even more disgusting to me is the fact that her mouth has had cocks in it. I wonder what it is, other than age, that turns a mouth a man would want to put his cock in into a twitching hole getting yogurt shoveled into it with a baby spoon.

At some point in this old cunt's life some guy was paying for her dinner, buying her presents, and being as nice and romantic as possible just so he could put his cock in that disgusting fucking hole.

On the plane—

There's a girl sitting next to me with red hair and perfect rock-hard C cups. She can't be more than nineteen and I'd love to know her name so I could see if it fits. I don't ask her even though she'd probably tell me, and it might even lead to a full-on conversation, which might lead to something else, like getting her number or taking her out to dinner. Instead, I just lean back, get a big whiff of her shampoo, and wonder if she could ever possibly know that I'll think about her for the next few weeks every time I jerk off. Probably not.

And I'm out like a light.

I'm still in a weird kind of dream when I get off the plane at LAX so I'm not sure if Trent Reznor walks past me at the Delta baggage claim. I am sure that the redhead is standing by me, and even though I don't have any bags to wait for, she does, so I pretend to.

I look at her luggage tag when she picks up her suitcase. Alyna Janson. It fits.

Satisfied, I go wait for twenty minutes to pay twenty dollars to ride a SuperShuttle back to my apartment in Westwood. Coincidentally enough, Alyna gets on the same SuperShuttle and tells the driver she's going to UCLA, two blocks from my house.

I stare at her without her knowing or caring until we get to her stop. When she gets out I don't make any effort to move out of her way, so she has to brush me with her ass, and she has a nice fucking ass.

When I get off the bus at my own stop I'm glad I never talked to Alyna. When I walk through my front door I wish I had. When I hit my bed, I'm glad I have a girlfriend I can fuck on a regular basis. When I wake up the next morning to a phone call begging me to spend my last days off going to the gym and shopping at Century City with her, I wish I didn't.

some chapter

Casey at the Gym

Casey has a fat ass. She's a pretty cute brunette with a completely normal upper body, just with a big fat ass attached. She knows it's fat and got a membership to my gym so she could go with me and "get cute tight buns." She even toyed with the idea of getting a personal trainer and she bought an exercise book called *The Daily Butt Regimen*.

So I'm sitting on the calf machine ready to put my head through the fucking mirror. Casey's across the gym, smiling at me, doing curls. For the past six months, since she started her ass-slimming campaign, all she's done is fucking curls and bench presses—and her ass shows it.

I've tried to get her to do squats with me, leg presses, quad extensions, hamstring machine, any fucking thing having even the most remote influence on the movement of muscles in her lower body, and she always says, "I think I'll just do some curls."

I finish my set and move to another part of the gym so I can't see her.

That night, after suffering through a TiVoed three-episode *Real World* marathon, I'm rewarded by her letting me fuck her doggie style. As I look down at her fat ass, I wonder if fucking her hard enough will have any kind of slimming or toning effect. Couldn't hurt.

chapter three

Century Fucking City

The one good thing you can always count on at Century City, and any place in this fucking city for that matter, is that there will always be a shitload of hot bitches with perfect bodies walking around. As chance would have it, I'm staring at one when my girlfriend says, "Do you wish I looked like that?"

I wonder if the three hours I've spent looking at shoes and other gay shit could possibly earn me one second of honesty with Casey. Probably not. Instead of answering her, I just look up at nothing in particular and say, "Do you smell pizza? I'm hungry."

On our way to the food court we pass a bookstore with a big line of middle-aged women, housewives mostly, some with kids, snaking out the front door. None of them are hot. They all seem like they're from the Valley or maybe Pasadena. I hate myself for being able to make the distinction. The window advertises that Marie Osmond is inside signing copies of her book *Behind the Smile: My Journey Out of Postpartum Depression*. I turn my head to ask Casey if she wants pizza, too, but she's already in line behind a woman who has a fat ass similar to her own and could easily be Casey's future self.

I'm pretty sure Casey knew about this and actually wanted to come to Century City just to see Marie Osmond, which means the fucking hours of looking at stupid shit were just insult to injury. Because of this, I kind of want to disappear into the food court and spend the rest of the day changing my phone number, but I decide it's not worth the effort of finding someone else to have regular sex with and get in line with my girlfriend.

Future Casey turns around and begins the following unsolicited conversation:

"Are you fans of Marie?"

Casey says, "I love her. I think it took so much courage to write about what she went through."

Future Casey says, "You know, a lot of women go through postpartum depression." She holds up her right hand like she's swearing on a Bible before she testifies, then she testifies, "Speaking from experience here. And I think this book is really going to help a lot of us. I mean it just makes me feel better to know that even somebody as important as Marie Osmond has felt what I felt."

I then end the conversation with this: "Maybe that woman in Houston who drowned all five of her kids should have read it."

Future Casey turns around and buries her nose in the latest issue of *Women's Health* magazine. Casey gives me an accusatory stare. I respond by saying, "I guess Marie can't help everyone." Casey responds by rolling her eyes and picking up the most recent issue of O from the magazine rack, which the bookstore has conveniently moved outside and stocked only with O and *Us Weekly*.

She reads it for the next fifteen minutes while we wait. I read it over her shoulder and these are the results:

Pictures of Oprah: Twenty-two (including her standard cover appearance).

"Articles" "written" by Oprah: Six (including the O magazine staple "What I Know for Sure," in which Oprah lies about how hard her life is and hammers home how much more spiritual she is than the average person).

Uses of the phrase "Self-realization": Ninety-four (in thirteen different "articles").

Ads for Oprah-related products: Seven (including one for Dr. Phil's show).

Paragraphs containing poorly veiled condescension: Four hundred sixty-three.

Impulses to ram the magazine up Oprah's cunt: One (that lasts for the entire fifteen minutes I stare at O).

The other conversations around us might as well be the same as the one Future Casey started with Casey, the main difference being that I can't stop any of the others with the uneasiness of honesty. I try to keep myself entertained by explaining to Casey the importance of the Nintendo Wii as a next-gen console actually being able to compete in the marketplace against the vastly more powerful Xbox 360 and PS3. She reopens O. So I decide to just stand there and not listen to the cackling around me.

This is what I hear: "Marie Osmond has amazing courage. . . . Marie Osmond is a genius writer. . . . This book should win an Oscar, or whatever the writing Oscar is. . . . The writing Oscar is the Nobel Prize. . . . She's a hero. . . . Yesterday Dr. Phil was giving women the courage to leave abusive relationships and lose weight at the same time. . . . Today I think the Dr. Phil show is about teaching women how to be independent. . . . Dr. Phil is probably a great husband. . . . Cloning and stem cell research is evil because they have to murder babies to do it. . . . If Oprah was sick or dying, it would be worth sacrificing one child to save her, though. . . . Carney Wilson wrote a courageous book about her lifelong battle with weight. . . . It took amazing courage to have her stomach surgically reduced to the size of a thumb."

The uneasy rage all of this creates in me starts out as something general, shapeless. But as it continues and we move up in line, Marie Osmond becomes the focus of everything I feel and the reason I feel it. I leer at her.

She smiles the samc smile every few minutes. She sips from the same lipstick-smeared Diet Coke can every few minutes. She gives the same genuinely concerned expression every few minutes. She checks the same clock on the back wall every few minutes. She makes the same $150 every few minutes.

I try to calm myself by thinking about the fact that someday this woman will die, when she says, "Who should I make this out to?" and we're standing a foot away from the courageous Marie Osmond.

Casey says, "Casey Childress, please," and continues with, "I really love your work and I'm a huge fan."

Osmond follows up with a concerned face and, "Well, I just hope this book has helped at least a few women out there."

I want to say something mean, something wrong, something that will make me feel like this entire day isn't a complete waste, but I know if I do Casey won't suck my dick until tomorrow at least, maybe even the next day. So I shut up and steal a quick peek down Osmond's shirt while she's signing the book. Not bad for an older bitch.

She looks back up at Casey, smiles, and says, "There you go, thanks." I picture myself behind her, pushing her head down on the table right in the middle of all her books and fucking her until she goes catatonic. I smile and say, "Thank you, Ms. Osmond." Then we leave.

Back at Casey's place, I kiss her and take off her shirt. "Aren't we frisky?" she says.

"No, I'm fucking horny and I want to fuck you right now," I whisper, knowing after a year of being in this relationship that whispering "fuck" in her ear makes her feel naughty enough to let me do anything I want to her. She unzips my pants as I sit down on her couch. She jerks me off a little before I push on her head and she gets the hint to stop fucking around and suck my cock. While she does, I look over at

Marie Osmond's smiling face on the cover of Casey's new book. I pretend Casey's mouth is Osmond's cunt and I try to hear Casey slurping as Osmond sobbing. Aside from Casey spitting my semen all over my stomach, which she always fucking does, it ends up ranking in my top five blow jobs of all time.

chapter four

Brunch

Casey's telling me that she doesn't like it when I come to her house drunk. She says, "Last night was like having sex with a different person."

I want to ask her if that's good or bad, but by the time the question gets to my mouth I'm thinking about the dream I had last night and Casey still has a lot more to say, so I never do.

The dream:

I'm walking around the halls of my old junior high trying to find my locker. I think it's on the second floor, but the school doesn't have a second floor. So I go to the principal's office to get a map and a piece of bubble gum, which for some reason I'm sure will help me. Once I get there, though, the office is really this comic book store I used to hang out in when I was a kid, and Alyna, the girl that sat next to me on the plane, is leaning up against a magazine rack reading an old issue of The New Mutants.

I say, "What's the deal? Where's my locker?"

She says, "I don't know." Then she kisses me with one of those dream kisses that make you think when you wake up you'll have been married to the person who kissed you for twenty of the happiest years of your life.

I get tipped off that this probably isn't real when my old family dog who died when I was ten walks in and says, "Do you guys have change for a five?"

At that point I was just a little too conscious to hold on to it and I woke up with that awful empty feeling you get when you realize the person who can make you happier than anything is a fucking dream.

Casey's chewing off the corner of a grilled cheese sandwich and I'm so sick of the fucking cows on the walls in this place and the bitchy waitress. I think I smell dirt but it's just the hippie-type girl next to me with blonde dreadlocks and a bent-up straw cowboy hat.

Casey says, "You don't like the cows? I think they're the cutest."

And I guess I must've said that last bit out loud. I wonder if the hippie cowgirl heard me, but she's not looking at me so fuck it.

I think very briefly about asking Casey what she thinks about all day. Instead I stare at our waitress's ass as she refills a butter tub and wonder if Oprah Winfrey sucks cock, or ever has for that matter.

some chapter

An Average Sunday

9:20 A.M. Wake up with a hard-on.

9:21 A.M. Start jerking off to the bonus gangbang on *Cum Guzzlers* DVD left in DVD player from last night.

9:24 A.M. About to shoot my wad, flip the TV to a TiVoed episode of *The View* I keep for just this purpose and get supreme satisfaction in imagining what any of the bitches from this show would think if they knew I just blew a load into a dirty pair of underwear while watching their program.

9:25 A.M. Watch MTV for an hour even though I've already seen everything aired in that hour.

10:25 A.M. Try in vain to crack the top ten online scores for Mutant Storm Reloaded in the Xbox 360 Arcade.

11:16 A.M. Take good shit.

11:22 A.M. Try Mutant Storm Reloaded again. Quit after getting blown up on level sixty-four.

12:36 P.M. Check e-mail. Take opportunity while online to download some porn. Best of seventeen downloads is a 1:15 clip with sound called pussstretch.mpg in which a woman inserts a vibrating dildo into her cunt while a guy fucks her from behind at the same time. Loop it on my Windows Media Player and jerk off.

12:50 P.M. Put on clothes and walk to the LA Fitness in Westwood. Think about the first time I fucked a mulatto girl named Mary Cook as I walk.

1:04 P.M. Flirt with hot bitch behind the desk at the gym. Imagine fucking her in the whirlpool next to the women's dressing room.

1:06 P.M. Hate lifting weights.

2:18 P.M. Walk to Quiznos. Flirt with hot college bitch while she makes my foot-long Italian on white. Imagine fucking her with her ass in the lettuce bin. Smile at three hot sorority bitches sitting at a table in the back while I eat.

2:33 P.M. Pass another hot college bitch on my walk back home. Say hi to her. Think about what it would be like to fuck her in my shower. Consider asking her if she'd like to fuck—no strings.

2:46 P.M. Take off clothes in preparation for shower. Jerk off standing up over the crapper thinking about fucking Alyna, the girl on the plane, doggie style. Blow load in toilet.

2:52 P.M. Take shower. Wonder what Casey's doing. Think about Casey fingering herself. Want a blow job. Wish I was still in college. Regret missed opportunities.

3:02 P.M. Think about getting a haircut. Wonder who will be the next Nirvana. Remind myself that one day the sun will destroy this planet so nothing really matters.

3:03 P.M. Lie in bed. Catch a faint whiff of Casey's pussy in my sheets. Realize the cunt smell is actually on my face. Take a deep breath.

3:05 P.M. Check empty mailbox.

3:06 P.M. Watch an old episode of *Martin* in which Snoop Dogg guest stars as himself and throws a house party in Pam's apartment. Martin and Gina are too busy arguing to make it to the party on time. When they finally get there, all they find is a note left by Pam, Tommy, and Cole explaining that they all went with Snoop to an after-party on his pimp jet.

3:31 P.M. Feel balls for lumps.

3:32 P.M. Get a hard-on. Jerk off to a disintegrated VHS copy of *Beautiful Black Fuckers*. Blow load to memory of Mary Cook in the sixty-nine.

3:38 P.M. Hook up the 8-bit Nintendo. Start to play Contra. Get bored. Really want to play Super Mario Bros. but can't find the cartridge. Turn my room upside down looking for it.

3:47 P.M. Find *Footloose* cassette I received from Lisa Franklin for fifth-grade birthday. Wonder what happened to Lisa. Imagine what she looks like now. Imagine titty-fucking her adult version. Think better of it. Imagine fucking her doggie style.

3:48 P.M. Play *Footloose* cassette. Imagine being back in the fifth grade. Wonder if anybody was fucking in the fifth grade. Wonder if I could have even gotten a hard-on in fifth grade. Try to remember the first time I got a hard-on. Can't.

3:50 P.M. Think about the girls I could have fucked in junior high.

3:53 P.M. Think about the girls I could have fucked in high school.

3:57 P.M. Think of all the hot bitches from high school that I never fucked who are now married. Wonder if I'll ever fuck a bitch who's unbelievably hot.

3:59 P.M. Wish I was famous.

4:00 P.M. Wish I was rich.

4:01 P.M. Decide not to make bed again. Check eBay for Street Fighter II arcade game. Bid $10.00 on 1983 child's-size medium Skeletor Halloween costume. Bid $12.50 on Hypercolor "like new" size large T-shirt. Bid $2.00 on naked lady lighter.

4:17 P.M. Log on to World of Warcraft Proudmoore server and play my Tauren Hunter. Farm gold in Burning Steppes because there's nothing else to do.

8:34 P.M. Lose connection to server. Get call from Casey. Receive command to go to her house.

9:06 P.M. Get to Casey's house. Force her to watch *UFC Unleashed* with me. Want to fuck the round card bitch.

10:01 P.M. Watch the news. Want to fuck the news bitch. Look at Casey. Wish she had tits like the news bitch.

10:37 P.M. Wonder if any bitch actually really likes to be titty-fucked. Probably.

10:40 P.M. Take off my clothes and go into Casey's bedroom.

10:42 P.M. Lie in Casey's bed naked. Watch MTV. Seen it all this morning. Watch it anyway.

11:00 P.M. Watch Leno/Letterman.

12:30 A.M. Watch Conan/Kimmel.

1:07 A.M. Get head.

1:16 A.M. Wish Casey was the round card bitch from UFC while I fuck her.

1:32 A.M. Bullshit way through overly emotional postsex conversation about future of relationship while trying to stay awake. Hope for memory of conversation to stick in case she ever references it again.

1:48 A.M. Hear I love you, say I love you.

1:52 A.M. Welcome dreamless sleep.

chapter five

Groundlings Party

After a phone conversation with my friend Todd in which he tells me to rent *The Gift* because Katie Holmes is nineteen in it and she shows her tits, which are slightly hangy but still great C cups, Casey calls me. She says, "My improv class is having a party tonight and it's on the west side so you have to drive."

I pick Casey up and realize that she looks better for this party than she did on our first date. I wonder if there's a guy in her Groundlings class she wants to fuck, or maybe has fucked already. I don't ask her.

At the party—

The place is nice, the booze is free, and to my surprise there are actually some pretty hot bitches roaming around. It seems tolerable. I see Casey talking to some people in the living room so I head to the opposite end of the house, where I approach the hottest bitch I can find and instigate the following train wreck:

"How's it going?"

"I'm Julie." She puts out her hand.

I shake it, say, "Nice to meet you," and notice she smells fucking great—clean.

"I haven't seen you in class. Are you in intermediate?"

"I'm actually not in Groundlings."

"Well, what do you do?"

"Nothing interesting or important."

She laughs one of those laughs that says *Will & Grace* is her favorite show. Then she says, "Oh, that's so funny. You must be in class . . . or maybe . . . are you a Groundling trying to come to this party on the DL? Coming here to scout? You know, I've gone through intro and basic and now I'm in intermediate and I didn't even have to repeat once. My teacher, Tim, said Phil Hartman is the only Groundling who never had to repeat a class. But I'm keeping my fingers crossed. Tim told me I'm kind of a cross between Victoria Jackson, Molly Shannon, and Ellen Cleghorne. What do you think? Here, I'll do one of my characters."

She puts on a bad Russian accent and says, "I try to git vith ze man from Amerika, but all he vants ees ze sex vith eighteen-yer-uld."

She bows. "What do you think? It's like a Russian mail-order bride who's too old and ugly to get an American guy interested in her."

"Ouch!" I grab my head and act like I got hit by something. I walk away from Julie and wind up in the kitchen with two other hot bitches who are having the following conversation:

Hot Bitch #1 says, "I think *MADtv* is having auditions."

Hot Bitch #2 says, "My character work isn't strong enough for that yet."

"Mine either. I'm thinking about taking some WOW classes."

"I heard those really help keep you sharp."

I decide it's time to insert myself with, "What's going on?"

I get the "fuck off" eyes from both of them.

Hot Bitch #2 says, "Who are you? Are you even in class?"

"No, I'm here with some friends."

Hot Bitch #1 says, "Who?"

I remember the teacher's name. "Tim."

Hot Bitch #2 changes her tune pretty fucking quick. "You know Tim?"

"Yeah. We're good friends."

Hot Bitch #1 says, "I'm Jenny. Jenny Gilmer."

Hot Bitch #2 says, "Sharon."

They take turns saying, "Has Tim said anything about me? Does he think I'm funny? Has he said who he's passing on to the next level?" Plus at least five more minutes of explaining why they're the funniest girls in their class and how they're going to join Phil Hartman as the only Groundlings who never had to repeat.

I want to get the fuck out and I can't think of anything better, so this is what they get: "I have to take a shit."

I walk away hoping Casey will talk to whoever the fuck she has to talk to so I can get out of here, go back to her house, and pretend to accidentally finger her asshole before I fuck her. I also decide to get completely drunk immediately and not talk to anyone else for the rest of the night.

Once I'm finally drinking scotch straight from the bottle and telling any girl who tries to start up a conversation with me that she's too fat to talk to, I find myself standing in front of a TV watching Conan O'Brien.

Some complete asshole says, "Conan is so passé. I mean really, he's like the Jim Carrey of late night."

Some other fuckhead says, "You're so right. I mean, the Triumph bit is played out." I break my rule about not talking to anybody with, "Hey, ass-eyes, all that money you're spending on Groundlings classes is really paying off, 'cause it sure is funny that you're criticizing Conan fucking O'Brien when you're just standing here in a fucking jacket like a turd."

Even as I'm saying this shit, I know it only makes vague sense at best and people are looking, so I tack on, "P.S. You're gay."

I don't know why I say the last part, but it gets some laughs, which are hushed pretty quickly, and all of a sudden I'm the drunk guy at the party who nobody knows. Where the fuck is Casey?

I turn to get the fuck out and stumble a little bit. I don't fall or anything, just a little drunken stumble, and Fucknose says, "Hey, why don't you try some walking lessons," which is retarded but of course gets big laughs from all his cronies. I fight the urge to piss all over the floor and I really want to say, "P.P.S. You're a fucking idiot," but I'm pretty sure I need to lie down. So I stagger off down some hallway, wondering how Casey can associate with these fucks and genuinely wishing she would take me back to her place and just hold me for a while, which makes me realize this is the most drunk I've been since college.

I find a room that's not a bedroom, but it's dark and it has a door I can close so I go in. There's a washer, a dryer, an ironing board, a shitload of unpacked boxes, and a girl that might as well be one of the bitches I talked to earlier passed out on the floor in the corner.

I lock the door behind me, leave the lights off, and hit the floor hard enough to wake the bitch up from her booze coma.

She says, "What took you so long? I thought you just had to go to the bathroom."

The five words she doesn't actually slur sound like mush by the time they get to my booze-soaked brain so I have no fucking clue what she just said. But when she starts unbuttoning my pants and licking my belly button, I'm pretty sure she thinks I'm somebody else. Even though the room's pitch black, I can tell it's spinning just before I pass out.

I come to and I'm kind of surprised by somebody licking my balls and jerking me off. I'm even more surprised by the fact that I'm wearing a rubber. For some reason I become horrified at the possibility that the tongue on my nuts belongs to a guy. I reach down and squeeze two very well-made tits unencumbered by any clothing and my mind's at ease. The room's spinning a little but it's kind of nice in conjunction with the blow job from a complete stranger.

I realize that I'm actually cheating on Casey by letting this bitch suck my cock. At first I think the complete absence of guilt is directly related to the amount of booze I've been drinking. But somewhere through the spinning haze a bright and strange ray of truth emerges. It's not the booze, it's the ease. I would probably cheat on Casey all the time if I had to put out as little effort to do it as I am right now, drunk or sober.

From my crotch I hear, "So you're going to move me to advanced, right?"

I am fucking clueless. I don't answer.

She stops. "Tim, you're gonna move me up if I do this, right?"

I've never met Tim but I bet his voice sounds something like this: "Yeah, keep going."

I'm pretty hammered and it takes what I estimate to be fifteen minutes to get anywhere near shooting a load. It's when I'm squeezing her tit with one hand and controlling the pace of her head bobs with the other that I feel her start to finger my asshole. It's a first for me and it doesn't feel good per se, but it's not as bizarre as I might once have thought. More than anything, it gives me an idea.

"You know I can pull some strings for you even after the next level if you're willing to do a little extra."

"Are you saying you can get me in Sunday Company?"

"What do you think?"

"Well, I guess you are one of the people who votes on it . . . what do you want me to do?"

Thirty seconds later I'm balls-deep in her asshole and she seems to like it, corroborating my suspicion that all women secretly like being ass-fucked. I tell her to talk dirty, so she says, "Oh yeah, fuck my ass. Fuck it harder." So I do for another few minutes, then I pull out, peeling the rubber off as I do so it's still hanging out of her asshole when I turn her around and shoot a load all over her face and in her mouth.

I lie back in the dark and start pulling my pants back up. She's wiping my semen out of her eyes with a towel she found in the dryer. Wanting to be faithful to Tim, who I can only imagine is a complete fucking asshole, I say, "Welcome to Hollywood."

She's working on a glob of cum stuck in her hair, wondering if Phil Hartman ever had to do this, when I go back to the party, which has started to die down. I'm getting some weird looks from people who all look semi-familiar to me. One guy looks at me and says, "Get lost in the toilet?" Then they all start laughing and I'm trying to piece together what happened before I fucked that girl in the ass, but I get nothing. So I decide it's probably some stupid fucking Groundlings inside joke and head out back.

I make it outside and find Casey without incident. She's talking to some guy, and when I come walking up she says, "Tim, this is my boyfriend."

I've got a huge smile on my face when I say, "It's great to finally meet you. I've heard so much about you, I feel like I already know you," and I shake his hand with the one I used to prime that girl's asshole before I fucked it.

All guys know the look of knowing you're about to get some pussy, and that's the one that's on Tim's face when he checks his watch and says, "Great, great to meet you. I was just telling Casey here that I was supposed to meet up with another student of mine a few minutes ago." He leaves.

I look over at Casey and she might as well be in junior high dreaming about marrying her fucking history teacher. I want to puke. Instead, I know the shit's going to hit the fan pretty soon, so I say, "Let's get outta here, go someplace where it's just us." I flash my best "I love you" smile and it drills through her adolescent fantasy about Tim.

"Okay, that sounds good. Let's go."

Casey's cats are watching us fuck and I can't help but wonder if that girl realized I wasn't Tim after the fact, but kept it to herself and sucked the real Tim's cock when he went in that room anyway.

Casey cums. I'm not even close and I'm incredibly bored so I fake it, look her in the eyes, say, "I love you," kiss her forehead, wait until she falls asleep, go in the bathroom, and jerk off to memories of the girl I butt-fucked a few hours earlier.

chapter six

My Gay Buddy

I have one gay friend. His name's Carlos and I've known him since college. We eat lunch every Saturday at the California Pizza Kitchen in the Beverly Center.

It's just such a Saturday and I'm sitting on a bench outside CPK flipping through an *LA Weekly* waiting for Carlos to show up. This girl sits down next to me and I notice she's hot as fuck. I further notice that she's more than just hot as fuck. She has some quality that makes me think I could live with her. She smiles at me.

I say, "How're you doing?"

"Fine."

I almost get in another sentence when Carlos shows up and says, "So you ready to have lunch with your favorite cocksucker?"

I want to explain to this girl that I'm not gay, that Carlos is just my gay friend, but she's already laughing and I notice that her tits are a little saggy. So I just get up and follow Carlos into CPK.

We sit down, order the same shit we always do, and Carlos starts up a conversation that's pretty much identical to a million we've had before. He wants to be an agent, but not at Paradigm, where he's currently an assistant. He always gets crushes on straight masculine guys. He's never going to find a fag who's masculine enough to satisfy him. And he rounds it out with some other shit about life not going the way he wants it to.

As the waiter walks away from the table after setting down our drinks, the following conversation takes place:

Carlos says, "I'd like him to plow my ass like a cabbage field."

"Tell him that the next time he comes over and see if it works."

"Hell, it wouldn't be the first time."

"What? You've just come out and told some guy that you want him to 'plow your ass' and then you go do it?"

"Yep."

"I don't fucking believe that."

"It's not the same as how you poor cunt-lickers have to deal with women. Think about it. If a woman came up to you and said she wanted to fuck your cock till it broke, you'd go home with her in a heartbeat, right?"

"Yeah."

"But a woman would never be that honest and no guy can say anything even close to honest to a woman if he ever wants to get laid. But if you just get rid of all that woman shit, all you've got left is two guys who want to fuck and have no problem telling each other as much."

"So in a bar you just go up to a guy and say, 'Let's fuck,' and within fifteen minutes you're back at one of your places fucking?"

"Not exactly. This is where the whole woman thing has its benefits. Once you straight assholes know there's going to be fucking, there's never any question about who's fucking and who's getting fucked. With two faggots, that's the only question. Usually before you even bring up the possibility of fucking, you ask, 'Are you a top or a bottom?'"

"What're you?"

"I'm a bottom all the way."

"So you let guys fuck you in the ass?"

"I beg them to. It's the only way I can cum."

"So you don't ever actually put your dick in anything? You don't even like getting your dick sucked?"

"I tried it once, but couldn't finish. I suck dick and take it up the ass and that's all I do."

"You must be pretty popular."

"Please, ninety percent of the faggots on this planet are bottom boys and most of 'em are far better looking than me."

"So most gay guys don't like to fuck, they want to be fucked?"

"Think about it, if we wanted to put our dicks in a hole, we could just get a girl. Speaking of, how're you and Casey doing?"

"Same old bullshit."

"Is that good or bad?"

"It's just . . . the same."

"I guess that's better than bad. Is she still doing Groundlings?"

"Yeah."

"You know, I met some guy at a party last week who said he was in Groundlings. I offered to suck his cock, but he was a complete bottom, too. That's usually how it works."

"So what happens with two bottoms?"

"The same thing that would happen if you met a girl who told you the only way she could get off was to strap on a dildo and fuck you in the ass and she would never suck your cock or let you fuck her . . . you never talk to each other again. Unless, of course, you're both drunk and horny and no other prospects are shaping up. Then you go home together, try to fuck each other with limp dicks, and then get out the dildos."

"So you use dildos on other guys instead of your own dicks?"

"I'm a fucking bottom, that's what I've been trying to tell you."

The waiter hears that last bit before he sets down our lunch. I think I see him flash Carlos a smile before leaving.

The rest of the lunch conversation is less interesting, mostly about

Reese Witherspoon's movies and mostly coming from Carlos. When we get the check there's another piece of paper with it that Carlos picks up, reads, and then shows me.

It reads, "I would love to plow your tight ass," followed by a number.

some chapter

Closure

I get an e-mail from Jenna.

It reads, "I don't know exactly how to tell you this, so I guess I'll just do it. I'm getting married to Mitch on Saturday.—Me."

Jenna was my longest relationship—four years. I'm pretty sure she was the only girl I ever really loved. She was going to move out to California with me after she graduated from college in Colorado so we could get married. Instead, the week of her graduation, she got arrested for stealing from Forever 21, where she was an assistant manager and apparently the ringleader of a scam in which she and fellow employees would take clothes that customers returned instead of noting the return and putting the merchandise back on the shelves as dictated by the Forever 21 employee handbook. The same week she told me she couldn't afford a place of her own so she moved in with her "friend" Mitch, who was the manager of a NASCAR Superstore in the mall. She dumped me a few weeks later. We haven't talked since.

I remember meeting Mitch and the only things that stand out are that he had fucked-up teeth and that he's a born-again Christian.

Strangely the e-mail doesn't surprise me that much. It doesn't bother me at first, but then I realize the concrete reality of the situation is that I will never fuck her again. I immediately turn off my computer and jerk off to memories of fucking Jenna in the ass in her parents' bed, her jerking me off as I shoot a load on her face, fucking her in her parents' swimming pool while they were inside with a prayer group, every load I ever shot down her throat, and the night I took her virginity. I try to convince myself that this is the last time I will ever think of Jenna. I immediately know I'll think about her again if for no other reason than she was the first girl I ever fucked in the ass, and that is one of my favorite memories.

chapter seven

I Don't Believe in Destiny

I'm walking back to my apartment through Westwood after having just come from the gym. As I pass a record store a Tori Amos poster catches my eye. I remember a girl in college who fucked me a few times because she saw my roommate's copy of a Tori Amos album lying on the floor and thought it was mine. She thought I was a sensitive guy who listened to that type of shit and to my surprise gave some of the best head I've ever had. I always kind of felt guilty for never paying Tori back.

Past the poster, through the window, I see something and almost shit my pants. Alyna the plane girl is working behind one of the registers. I decide to buy a fucking Tori Amos album.

As I walk in, I'm immediately hit with a wave of panic. I don't know if I should act like I remember her from the plane or if I shouldn't. What should I do if she remembers me? I busy myself by walking over to a listening station, but it's broken.

I browse the DVD section.

Fuck it, I walk up to the counter, straight to her.

"Do you guys have a new release section or something?"

"Yeah, it's over there."

I walk over in the direction she pointed without a doubt in my mind that she remembers me. I wander around for a few minutes, away from the new releases, until I find some Tori Amos CDs. I take one, pretend to look around at some other shit and see if I can catch her checking me out. I can't.

I go back up to the register and toss the disc on the counter. She picks it up and looks at it, then looks at me.

"Are you really into this?"

I don't know what the fuck to say. "Uh, yeah, I like her stuff, why?"

"All of her music sounds the same."

"Whose doesn't?"

"Good point."

She rings me up and that's our first conversation.

That night Casey comes over and sees the unopened CD lying on my couch.

"I never knew you liked Tori."

She unwraps the CD and starts playing it. I wonder if she ever fucked a guy based on his musical preference.

Later that night she tells me that she's just not in the mood for sex. For the first time since we've started fucking, this doesn't bother me. Casey curls up next to me and falls asleep in my arms without touching my dick at all and it doesn't bother me. I wonder what Alyna's ass looks like when you fuck her doggie style and spread it apart a little bit, and I fall asleep.

chapter eight

Casey's New Diet

We're at Johnnies New York Pizzeria on Sunset because it's one of Casey's favorite places to eat. To be fair, the rolls are fucking amazing, and we did see Lara Flynn Boyle there once. So I'm content.

Casey's retelling me a joke she says she got forwarded to her by her Groundlings teacher. The same joke was sent to me by Casey herself a few days ago in an e-mail that explained she had come up with the joke herself, which I knew to be untrue even then because it had already been forwarded to me by my mom.

Nonetheless, Casey is butchering the joke, and even though I already know what's coming, I let her continue, and when she retells me the punch line, slightly botched, I laugh convincingly enough to assure a decent prefuck blow job tonight.

After what seems like a fucking eternity of her telling a drawn-out story about losing her dad's credit card in the Beverly Center Gap, Casey finally gets up to go to the bathroom. Just as she leaves, the waiter puts our plates down, giving me the perfect opportunity to make my move.

About a month and a half ago I was watching some late-night TV after having jerked off twice in a row to a videotape I found in my closet of me fucking my high school girlfriend, Katy. Flipping through the channels, I was blessed with an infomercial for a product called Bloussant.

Bloussant is a pill taken daily that is guaranteed to enlarge tits by at least one cup size. Seventy-four dollars and fourteen business days later my own two-month supply of Bloussant arrived in the mail. I crushed up all the pills into a powder that I've been mixing into as many of Casey's meals as I can. I've been doing this for about a month and so far the results could be better.

I decide to increase her dosage and spoon out two heaping mounds of the stuff from the Ziploc Baggie I have in my right back pocket. An old guy sitting next to me notices but doesn't give any reaction. I mix it in the best I can and decide it would be a good move to put a third spoonful in her Diet Coke.

I'm concentrating too hard on making sure the Bloussant is completely dissolved to notice that Casey's come back from the bathroom and is standing at the table watching me stir her drink.

She says, "What're you doing?"

Something quick, nonchalant, believable: "I thought I saw a fly or something in your drink."

"Then I'll just get the waiter to bring me a new one when he comes back."

"No, no. You don't need to do that. There wasn't really a fly. I just thought there was. It must have been the ice. C'mon, sit down, let's dig in."

She looks at me like I'm semi-insane and for a split second I wish I was so I could be honest enough with her to tell her that I've been slipping an unproven breast-enhancing drug into her food and drink because I think her tits are too small and I was stirring her Diet Coke to make sure it had completely dissolved. But her look fades as she sits down, spreads her napkin across her lap, and takes a huge bite of fettuccine Alfredo–Bloussant. Her reaction to a strange taste is nonexistent.

I grab her tits much more than I normally would that night as we fuck in an attempt to feel any kind of progress at all. She says, "Hey, calm down, they'll last longer if you don't rip them off." I'm surprised at how genuinely funny I think this is while my dick's buried in her pussy. But the distraction's not enough to keep me from thinking that at her current increased dosage, I only have enough Bloussant left for about a week and a half. If I don't see better results by then, I'll have to buy two more shipments and further increase her intake. This may mean I'll be forced to take up cooking to learn how to mask the taste.

some chapter

Communication Is the Foundation of Any Good Relationship

In Casey's car on the way to the beach I'm staring out the window wondering if Alyna knows how to suck cock when Casey starts the following conversation with me:

Casey says, "Yesterday I get this e-mail from Lem. He asks me if I was invited to Eliza's party. And, of course, I was, but he wasn't. So I e-mail him back that I was. Then he e-mails me back and asks if I can forward him the invitation just so he can see who was invited. I mean, what is he thinking? So I e-mail back that I'd forward it to him, but I told him if he doesn't get invited he can't go. You know, like don't use this e-mail that I'm about to forward you as an invitation if you don't get one yourself. Then he e-mails me back that he's all pissed off at me because how dare I think that he would try to come to a party that he wasn't invited to and blah, blah, blah—and I'm trying to IM with Nancy at the same time to see what she's wearing to the party, but his e-mails keep popping up. I was so afraid I was accidentally going to send him an e-mail about what he's wearing to the party after I pretty much already told him not to come. I couldn't believe he got so mad when I told him not to show up unless he got his own invitation. Who does that? Who comes to a party without an invitation? I mean, he shouldn't be surprised that he doesn't get invited to things. He just doesn't know what it's all about, you know? I mean, can you believe that?"

I say, "Huh-uh."

She says, "Then he sends me another e-mail where he's mad because Joan got invited and he didn't. I mean, of course Joan's going to get invited. That doesn't mean he is. You know, it's like he thinks Greg still owes him something or something. If he wasn't so socially retarded he might get invited to more parties. And plenty of people think that, but it's like, who's going to be the one to tell him? So anyway, the last e-mail he sends me is all like crazy and pissed off about the fact that he hasn't been invited to the last two parties and he asked me to e-mail Eliza and ask her to e-mail him an invitation. Can you believe that?"

I say, "Huh-uh."

She says, "I didn't even write him one back. If he's that desperate to go to her party, then he can ask her himself. Can you imagine me e-mailing her to ask if she'll invite Lem to her party? Oh, yeah, and he asks me if I have Shawna's phone number. Hello, Shawna moved to New York like four months ago. If you don't have her number, it's because she doesn't want you to have it. I mean, seriously, learn to take a hint. And he sends me this thing that he sent to like thirty other people about his stupid jazz trio playing somewhere in North Hollywood. North Hollywood, can you believe that?"

I say, "Huh-uh."

She says, "Who plays in North Hollywood? Nobody good. I'm sure nobody'll go. I kind of feel sorry for him. But it's like it's his own fault, you know. He just doesn't get the whole thing. So then I send Eliza an e-mail saying basically watch out for an e-mail from Lem inviting himself to her party. He's been asking around about why he wasn't invited. Then she e-mails me back saying that Lem already called her at work and wanted to know what the deal was—if Eliza had lost his e-mail address or something. She told him that she was sorry and she must have lost his e-mail otherwise he would have been invited, but the party was only open to the first fifty people who RSVPed because her place is kind of small. Then she told him that she'd definitely make sure he was on the list for her next party, but there's no way. Now he'll never get invited to anything again because everybody knows that he tried to invite himself to this party. I just—I mean, can you imagine being like that?"

I say, "Huh-uh."

An old No Doubt song comes on the radio. She doesn't say anything while it plays. I think about Alyna's ass and what she's like after sex. When the song's over Casey says, "Oh, yeah, my sister had her baby yesterday and my parents bought me a ticket to go home and see her. So I'll be gone for a few days next week."

I say, "That's great."

chapter nine

Burbank Strip Club

I'm at Todd's house in Toluca Lake. We've been playing Madden for a few hours and drinking heavily. After his fourth defeat he says, "Dude, let's go see some titties."

Twenty minutes later we're driving over some train tracks at a nondescript location in Burbank and pulling into the parking lot of a strip club I never knew existed.

We sit down, order the first of our two-drink minimum and look to stage one, where a moderately attractive girl with no ass grinds her crotch in the air to the beat of a far-past-its-prime Limp Bizkit song.

I say, "I think I'm going to ask that girl out."

"That girl from the record store?"

"Yeah."

"Like on a date?"

"Yeah."

"Why?"

"I think about her constantly."

"Do what you gotta do."

Two strippers, both far below par as strippers go, approach us about some lap dances. I'm hesitant, but then they explain their rates.

This pudgy Asian stripper says, "You get three songs for twenty dollars."

I say, "Why so cheap?"

Her partner, a pock-faced white girl with some kind of Scandinavian accent, says, "It's three-for-one night." Then she leans in and licks my ear. I'm almost repulsed by the idea of a three-for-one rate on lap dances, but the bitch is already sitting in my lap. Fuck it.

The pock-faced white girl has her ass in my face while the chubby Asian girl rubs her tits on Todd's head.

Todd comes out from under her tits, looks at me, and says, "Dude, what about Casey?"

I stop staring at this stripper's asshole long enough to look at Todd and say, "What about Casey?"

"How're you gonna take that record store girl on a date without Casey finding out?"

My stripper flips around and mashes her little hard tits in my face. I say, "Casey's leaving town for a few days."

The Asian bitch rolls her head around in Todd's crotch. He says, "Lucky."

The pock-faced bitch breathes on my cock through my pants. I say, "Yeah, I know. But I don't even know this girl's phone number or anything."

The Asian bitch takes Todd's hands and puts them on her slightly dimpled ass. He says, "Dude, you know where she works."

The pock-faced bitch starts semi–jerking me off through my pants. I say, "But I don't know when she works. I can't just hang out in the store all day."

The Asian bitch does this crab-type maneuver that has her crotch gyrating right under Todd's nose. He says, "Dude, just ask somebody who works there when she works."

The pock-faced bitch matches her partner. I try to sniff her cunt, but it's masked by the stripper smell. I say, "Good idea."

The Asian bitch puts her hands under Todd's shirt and presses her face into his cock. He says, "No shit."

Our conversation ends and our drinks come. The strippers get off us for a few seconds so we can dig our money out of the pockets they've been rubbing their asses all over. I feel a little ripped off by the convenient hiatus created by the waitress's arrival. The waitress leaves and the bitches get back to work.

Some Tool song and a Linkin Park song finish out my three-for-the-price-of-one session. The highlight is when the pock-faced stripper accidentally slips off the side of the chair, hits the ground, and says, "Fuck, I hate these fucking shoes," with no trace of the Scandinavian accent.

chapter ten

Stevie

I'm at the Gap in Westwood with Casey watching her look at clothes.

She says, "Do you think I should get a Gap credit card?"

"Sure."

"I mean, I think you get ten percent off and you can use it like a normal credit card. Should I get one?"

"Yes."

"I don't know if I should though. Should I?"

"Do it."

"I'll think about it. I need to look around some more. If I find something that I like, I might get the card, too. I'm going to try some things on."

I wait until she takes an armload of clothes into the dressing room and then walk across the street to the record store where Alyna works.

She's not in the store, but a kind of overweight middle-aged guy with glasses and a crew cut is. His name tag reads STEVIE—MANAGER.

I say, "Excuse me."

"How can I help you?"

"Do you know Alyna?"

"Yes, I do."

"Do you know when she works next?"

"Yes, I do." He points at his name badge. "I *am* the manager." He laughs.

"Right. So when is she supposed to work next?"

"Are you a family member?"

"No, I'm—a friend."

"Then I'm afraid I can't tell you."

"Why not?"

He points to his name badge again. "Like I said, I *am* the manager, and as the manager I have a duty to my employees. I can't just go around giving out their personal information to every stranger who asks for it, now can I?" He laughs again.

"It's not personal information."

"I'm sorry, I can't help you."

"Well, can I leave a message for her?"

He thinks about it. "I suppose that would be all right."

"Do you have a piece of paper?"

He gives me a promotional flyer for Justin Timberlake's new record.

"And a pen?"

He gives me one.

I write down something short, and put my phone number next to it. I fold it up, write Alyna's name on the outside, and hand it back to Stevie.

He unfolds it and starts reading it out loud. "Alyna, I bought the Tori Amos record from you a few days ago. We kind of had a conversation about it. I was wondering if you might want to get dinner sometime. Call me."

Stevie looks at me, then rips the paper in half and tosses it in the trash.

"What're you doing?"

"You said you were her friend, which is clearly not the case. I try to create a safe and comfortable work environment here and I will not have my employees harassed during the course of their workday."

"Are you kidding?"

"Sir, if you do not wish to make a purchase, I'm afraid I'm going to have to ask you to leave my store."

"It's not your store, Stevie."

I leave without incident, pissed.

I slip back into the Gap just in time to wait for another thirty minutes before Casey comes out of the dressing room and buys a sweater with her new Gap card.

As we walk out of the Gap, Casey says, "Hey, let's go in that music store. My No Doubt CD got stuck in Jen's CD player and she scratched it trying to get it out. I need a new one."

"You go ahead. I'll be next door looking at video games."

I browse the used section while I'm positive Stevie is next door drooling over my girlfriend's tits and taking way too long to help her find her No Doubt CD.

That night as Casey and I are in the sixty-nine and I'm staring into her asshole, I wonder if Alyna will be working at the record store tomorrow. I wonder if my ripped-up note will still be in the trash can by the front desk. I wonder if she might see her name on it and pull it out. I wonder if she'd even remember who I was anyway.

some chapter

Scarface Part 1

I'm sitting in a bar called Goldfinger after getting a phone call from Todd promising me that at least three hot bitches he knows from college who are all horny and drunk will be there. After my third beer and Todd's sixth assurance that they must be on their way, I'm pretty sure there might never have been any hot bitches, and I'm positive if they do exist they're not showing up here tonight.

I get up to go get another drink, and when I come back Todd has somehow managed to fill our booth with not the promised three hot bitches, but four average-looking bitches. I conclude that these are not the girls he was originally talking about, but I don't really care. I sit down and learn the following:

The taller bitch with reddish hair is named Leslie Leonard and she's visiting from Virginia. Two of the brunettes' names make no impression on me and I don't remember them even as they tell me, but I do latch on to the fact that they're sisters and Leslie is their cousin. The third brunette is Asian and semi-hot from what I can see, until the candle flicker at our table bounces off a nasty fucking hairlip. I think she gives her name as Amy, but I immediately give her the name Scarface in my head.

After they're done telling us whatever their stories are, Scarface says with a lisp that isn't altogether unattractive, "Do you guys have girlfriends?"

It's a weird question. Todd says, "No." I don't say anything. Scarface says, "Cool."

I'm strangely attracted to her weird lip. I wonder if she's had to develop some super cocksucking technique to compensate for her deformity. I wonder if she can even suck cock at all. Maybe she can't suck cock so she's had to expand her sexual repertoire to keep men interested. I picture myself fucking her in the ass and her genuinely enjoying it because she has to, because she knows that her openness to things other women aren't is the most and only attractive quality she has.

Leslie Leonard says, "So have you guys seen any good movies lately?"

Todd says, "Movies are pretty gay right now. I saw the last UFC though."

One of the sisters says, "What's UFC?"

Todd says, "Ultimate Fighting Championship."

The conversation is dead until Scarface says, "Is that like boxing?"

I wish the beer I'm drinking was Scotch.

Scarface keeps on talking, "Boxing is pretty cool. I don't mind watching that."

Scarface keeps going on about how much she can tolerate boxing, even more than watching football, and I keep watching her mouth move and wondering if there's any way I could actually get her to suck my cock tonight. She seems kind of stupid but that doesn't give me enough of a read to devise a game plan. I decide to wait it out, let her talk, let her get comfortable with me, and see where it goes.

Two hours later I'm more drunk than I wanted to be and Scarface's lip doesn't look abnormal to me at all. I don't know if it's because I'm drunk or because I've stared at it for so long that it just seems normal. They shut down the bar and our whole group goes outside.

I look over and see Todd kissing Leslie Leonard, which makes me realize there must have been an entire part of the night that I somehow missed while I was staring at Scarface's lip, which I'm still doing when it moves and she says, "So are you gonna give me your number or what?"

The alcohol and the hypnotic spell her lip has cast on me slow my mind to the point of not being able to produce a fake number. I give her my real one, not remembering even as I say it to find the strength to change a single digit.

Scarface gives me a hug and for the first time all night I notice her body, which is nice. Hard little tits and a flat stomach. I wonder if she works out at home or if she braves a public gym with her lip. I wonder if she gets a Jamba Juice after she works out like I do sometimes and I also wonder if she uses a straw or if she even has the ability to use a straw.

She hops in a car driven by one of the two sisters, as does Leslie Leonard, leaving Todd and me standing on the sidewalk. Todd says, "Dude, that bitch gave me her number. She's only in town for another four days and she gave me her number. It's fucking on."

I didn't know at the time I decided to recognize her as Scarface if Todd did the same, but when he says, "So what happened with you and Scarface?" I realize he did. This also makes me realize that most guys' default nickname for a bitch with any facial deformity is probably Scarface.

I say, "I think I gave her my number."

"Holy shit. Your real number?"

"Yeah."

"Why?"

"I don't know."

"Dude, her face is fucked up."

"I know."

"You think she'll call you?"

"I don't know."

"Holy shit."

"I know."

chapter eleven

I'm Starting to Believe in Destiny

I'm in the Beverly Center pet store with my gay buddy, Carlos. We just finished our weekly lunch and he's thinking about buying a dog. There are two thirty-something flaming fags next to us also thinking about buying a dog. One of them is holding a baby pug.

Fag 1 says, "I just don't know if I should get him. I mean, I'm leaving town for two months. What would I do?"

Fag 2 says, "I'll watch him for you."

Fag 1 says, "You would?"

Fag 2 says, "Of course. But he's so expensive, are you sure you want to get him?"

Fag 1 looks at the price on his cage. He says, "Thirteen hundred. That's not too expensive for me."

Fag 2 says, "Ooh, you're so naughty."

Then Fag 1 slaps Fag 2 on the ass and says, "You know it."

Carlos nudges me and says, "Let's get the fuck out of here."

As we leave the pet store and head to EB Games, Carlos says, "I fucking hate fags who're like that."

"Like what?"

"You know, all flaunting their money and their asses in public. I mean, please, who wants to hear that you can waste thirteen hundred dollars on a fucking dog? And who doesn't know that all homos have money because we have no women or children to suck us dry? And once you get out of college, who still slaps another guy on the ass? I need a fucking straight man who's willing to just let me suck his dick and who'll fuck me in the ass every once in a while without all the bullshit."

He bats his eyelashes at me.

"As much as I like blow jobs, I only like 'em when they come with tits."

"I'm not against implants."

He laughs at his own joke as we walk into EB Games.

I walk to the back of the store and look through their rummage bin, which is usually filled with old Sega Genesis and Super Nintendo games.

I've been looking for a game called Super Populous since the eighth grade. In the game you play a god who controls a population of people. The computer plays a rival god controlling its own population. The object of each level is to raise your population to such a large number that it completely destroys the opposing god's population. Each level takes roughly forty-five minutes to an hour to beat. There are 999 levels. After its release in 1990, it was rated the worst game of the year by several gaming magazines. One even rated it the worst game ever made. As a result, no store carried it for more than a month after it was released. So I had resigned myself to renting it from the only video store in town that carried it in the hopes of one day beating it.

Over the course of several rentals, I had progressed to the eighty-seventh level. One weekend while trying to rent it again, I was notified that it had not been returned and was thought to be stolen.

Since that day I've looked in any and every used game section I've come across. I've looked on eBay, I've looked at garage sales, I've even flipped through the classified ads every once in a while in the hopes of finding a video game collection for sale. Now, in the upper left part of the bin, right on top of the pile in this particular EB Games, is Super Populous for $2.99.

I'm almost catatonic with disbelief. A quest that has consumed multiple years of my life has finally and unexpectedly ended.

"How's that Tori Amos CD?"

Alyna Janson is standing in front of me holding a DS Lite.

"I actually haven't listened to it yet."

"I thought you were a big Tori fan."

"Not that big."

She looks at Super Populous in my hand. She says, "What's that?"

"Super Populous."

She doesn't know what it is or that my holding it means the end of a fifteen-year search.

I say, "Do you want to get dinner with me sometime?"

"Sure."

She takes a pen and paper out of her purse, writes down her number, and hands it to me. She says, "Here's my number, give me a call and we can hash out the details."

I take her number, put it in my back pocket, and say, "Okay."

She walks up to the counter to buy the DS Lite. I assume she's buying it for a brother or friend. She's wearing a pair of tight jeans that make her ass look slightly better than I remembered it. I pretend to look through the used game bin some more so I don't have to make eye contact with her again and possibly start up a clumsy and unnecessary conversation after just having successfully asked her on a date.

Carlos comes over to me and says, "Did you just ask that girl on a date?"

"Yeah."

"You little fucker. Are you and Casey still together?"

"Yeah."

"Then what the fuck are you doing?"

"I don't really know."

"You just saw some girl you wanted to fuck and asked her out or what?"

"No. I've seen her before. I saw her on a plane, and then I saw her in a record store. She sold me a CD. I constantly think about her."

"I guess I'm not the one to be giving you a lecture on fidelity. God knows I've fucked around on half of West Hollywood. But you better be fucking careful. Shit like this always blows up in your face."

I pay for Super Populous and we leave the Beverly Center.

When I get home I jerk off thinking about the possibility of fucking Alyna on our first date. I wonder if she's ever fingered herself while thinking about me.

some chapter

Scarface Part 2

I've been playing Halo 2 campaign mode for the past four hours on Legendary difficulty. I'm having trouble with the part where you have to pilot a Ghost around while a giant Covenant walker robot is decimating the city. The Covenant Ghosts do too much damage and there are too many of them. The phone rings. I answer it without stopping my game and hear a vaguely familiar lisp. It's fucking Scarface, who begins the following conversation:

"I had a really good time meeting you and your friend Todd when we were all out the other night."

"Uh-huh . . ."

"Did you?"

"Uh . . . sure."

"Cool. So what are you up to right now?"

"Uh . . . I'm playing Halo."

"Cool. What's that?"

"A video game."

"Cool. I love video games. I'm awesome at Tetris. You ever play Tetris?"

"Not really."

I have a bead on an enemy Ghost and my plasma cannon is fully charged. Before I pull the trigger I pretend Scarface is piloting the Covenant ship. As I blow him out of the air, I see his body falling down to the ground below.

Scarface keeps talking, "Hey, what kind of music are you into?"

"Uh . . . all kinds, I guess."

"Cool. Me too. I listen to pretty much everything."

What must be forty-five seconds pass and all I hear on the other end of the phone is air blowing in and out through Scarface's deformed lip. I try to ignore it as I mop up some more Covenant ships.

Then she says, "So do you date much?"

"Not too much."

"Yeah, same here. But when you do go on dates, what kind of stuff do you like to do?"

"Eat, I guess."

"Yeah, that's a really good thing to do on a date. Where do you like to eat?"

"I don't know, depends on what I'm in the mood for that day."

"Yeah, it totally does depend on that. Do you ever get in the mood for Italian food?"

"Uh . . . yeah, sure."

"I love Italian food."

There's another long pause during which I've managed to land my severely damaged Ghost and pick up an entirely new one to continue fighting.

She says, "Maybe we could go get something to eat at that Italian place in the Grove sometime soon if you're not busy."

I do a dive roll to avoid a salvo of glowing plasma rounds from an enemy ship and then say, "Uh . . . I'm not sure that's the best idea."

"Oh, oh, okay . . . cool. Well, I've got your number. Maybe I'll give you a call some other time."

Before I can say anything she hangs up and I find myself feeling genuinely bad for Scarface, bad enough to pause my game. I think for a few seconds about Scarface and how she must have similar conversations with guys all the time. I think about star-sixty-nining her and taking her up on the offer. She might be happy enough to have a date that she'd suck my dick or let me fuck her in the ass. I jerk off as I imagine her sucking my cock and I cum as I imagine blowing my load all over her deformed lip.

I use a paper towel from the kitchen to clean myself off and then unpause my game.

chapter twelve

Plans

I make specific plans not to go to Casey's house so I can call Alyna to set up our date. I've tried to prepare myself so I don't sound like a retard on the phone, but when I dial the number she gave me at EB Games and Stevie answers, all my preparation dissolves. I immediately wonder why she gave me her work number instead of her home number.

I say, "Is Alyna there?"

Stevie asks, "Who's calling?"

"A friend."

Surprisingly, Stevie gives me no shit and gets Alyna. When she gets on the phone I want to ask her why she gave me her work number, but I decide not to push the issue. It's not that relevant.

She says, "Hey, how've you been?"

I say, "Fine."

"So where are you taking me?"

My call waiting beeps. I don't want to answer it, but I can't help myself. I say, "Can you hang on one second?"

"Okay."

I switch over. It's Casey. She wants me to come over despite the fact that we've already decided to not see each other tonight. I'm very quickly faced with the fact that to get her off the line with any expedience, I have to promise to see her tonight. So I do. She says she loves me and I tell her I'll see her tonight before hanging up on her and switching back over to Alyna.

I say, "Sorry about that. So what kind of food do you like?"

"All kinds. Why don't you surprise me."

"Okay."

"And you can pick me up at eight-thirty on Friday night. That's my night off."

"Okay."

Then she gives me her address.

"See you then."

"Okay. See you then."

"Bye."

She hangs up before I can return the good-bye.

That night at Casey's house, I purposely cum in her mouth while she's giving me a standard foreplay blow job that should have led to sex. I don't apologize.

chapter thirteen

A Call from Casey's Mom

A few nights later I'm at Casey's house. She promised me she was horny and if I got to her house as fast as I could, she'd be waiting for me naked on her bed. We haven't fucked in a few days and she's leaving town tomorrow, so I accepted her offer.

Casey's lying on her bed, as she promised, but she's fully clothed and talking to her mom on the phone. Occasionally I can hear Casey say one of the following things: "I don't know. How am I supposed to know? I guess. No, you're right. I never thought about it like that. I will."

I'm sitting on her couch watching an old episode of *Who's the Boss* in which Tony Danza gets pursued by his overly aggressive high school girlfriend who just wants to have a fling for old time's sake. And although Tony really wants to fuck her, he can't stop thinking about Angela.

Who's the Boss ends and Casey's still on the phone. I find nothing to eat in her refrigerator, then go to the bathroom to piss.

When I lift up the toilet lid there's already piss in the bowl, and I'm reminded that in an effort to conserve water Casey never flushes after she pisses. There's something slightly unsettling about my piss mixing with her piss. When I flush I hear Casey say, "Only if it's brown."

I ignore her and go back to the living room, where I settle in for an episode of *Family Ties* in which Michael J. Fox takes amphetamines so he can study for a test without knowing the serious harm he could be doing to himself. It's just getting to the part that they use in the opening credits where a speed-wired Michael J. Fox slides across the floor in a rolling chair, when Casey steps right in front of the TV.

I try to look around her, but Michael J. Fox has already rolled across the floor. I missed it.

I notice she's not talking on the phone anymore when she says, "Sorry. She called right after I called you."

"That's okay."

I get up and start kissing her neck as I unzip her pants.

"Hang on."

"What?"

"I want to talk about something first."

"I thought you said you were horny."

"I was."

"But not now?"

"I just got off the phone with my mom."

"So?"

"She was asking me if we were ever going to get married."

"So?"

"So are we?"

I wish I would have left work ten minutes earlier so I wouldn't have been there when Casey called, or that I had just jerked off in the first-floor bathroom so the lure of fucking her wouldn't have been so strong. I wish a pot of scalding water was on the stove so I could dunk my head in it.

I can't talk. I just stand there.

She says, "Well . . . have you ever even thought about it?"

I can't think. I just open my mouth. "No."

"You've never even thought about us getting married?"

"No."

"We've been dating for like over a year."

"Right."

"And you haven't ever even given it the slightest thought? Like what I'd look like in a wedding dress?"

For the first time in my life, I imagine Casey in a wedding dress. She actually probably would look good from the front.

"No. Have you?"

"Of course. I love you."

My involuntary reactions come back to me. "I love you, too" crawls out of my mouth.

"Then why wouldn't you think about us getting married?"

"Why are you bringing this up now? What did your mom say to you?"

"She wanted to know if we were thinking about getting married yet or like thinking about having kids."

"Kids?" Is this a fucking joke?

"She had me when she was twenty."

"Kids?" It's not a fucking joke.

"My sister just had a baby and my mom wants me to give her grandchildren, too. I don't think that's so bad."

Her cats are sitting on the coffee table watching us argue. I wish they were watching us fuck.

I have to get out of this. I say, "Do you want to go get a sandwich?"

"What?"

"I didn't eat before I came over here. Do you want to go get a sandwich?"

"What are you talking about?"

"I want to get a sandwich."

"Are you like trying to change the subject or something?"

"No, I just, I'm just hungry."

She gets really pissed. She stomps off into her bedroom and slams the door shut. Her cats are still sitting on the coffee table just staring at me.

I'm afraid to knock on her door because I know the marriage conversation will have to be resolved. So I sit back down on the couch and finish watching *Family Ties*. I wonder how many eighteen-year-old hardbodies Michael J. Fox fucked in his prime—before Parkinson's, before marriage.

I watch TV for the next few minutes, during which I formulate my apology and the quickest route of conversation that will lead me to fucking. I watch a little bit of a soft-core porno on Cinemax called *A Rock and a Hard Place*. I contemplate jerking off in Casey's living room and then going home, but I ultimately decide against it. It turns out to be a good decision, as Casey comes out of her room ready to start up the conversation again.

She says, "So are you ever going to apologize?"

I don't think I've done anything wrong. I say, "Of course. I just thought you needed some time to yourself. I didn't want to interrupt you before you were ready to fully talk about this whole thing."

"Well, now I'm ready."

I take a deep breath and try to look like I care. I say, "What you said earlier just caught me by surprise. I came over here thinking about one thing and then your mom called and I ended up getting another. You know how us guys think."

"Yeah, like rocks."

"I know. I'm sorry."

"So then what do you think about the whole us getting married thing?"

This question inspires me to create the following masterwork: "Of course I've thought about us getting married. It's not like I don't see us together in the future. I guess what I meant was that I never even questioned whether or not we'd be married so I never really gave it much thought. It's just something that I kind of take as a given."

That one got her. She smiles and says, "So you think we'll get married?"

"Someday . . . in the future."

She sits down next to me and puts her arms around my neck. She says, "I knew you'd thought about it. You must have just been confused. Like you said."

"Right."

"And now that you've had some time to clear your thoughts, you realize that we should get married."

"Sure . . . at some point."

She squeezes me and kisses my cheek. She says, "I love you."

"I love you, too."

She pulls away a little bit and looks me in the eyes. She says, "So then we're basically engaged, right?"

"Uhh . . ." The only sound I can hear is the blood pounding against the back of my eyes. I'm dazed. She must take my slack-jawed stupor to mean yes because she hugs me tight and says, "I love the feeling of being engaged."

Dazed becomes paralyzed. I wish a plane would crash into Casey's living room.

She pulls back again and stares at me, this time with a look in her eye that I haven't seen since we first started dating, and she says, "You know what we should do to celebrate our engagement?"

I want to get the fuck out of her house and celebrate by wrapping my car around a telephone pole.

She says, "We should make love."

She insists on fucking missionary style so we can look into each other's eyes. She keeps holding my face and saying she loves me as I'm trying to fuck her hard enough to erase the memory of this entire night. She's nowhere close to cumming and I don't care because she keeps trying to hug me as we're fucking and she won't stop telling me how much she loves me.

I'm about to blow my load so I pull out and shoot it all over her stomach and tits, knowing that I'll get at least a little break from her "I love you" barrage while she goes to the bathroom to clean up.

I'm almost asleep when she comes back from toweling down. She snuggles up beside me and forces me into the spoon position.

Again she says, "I love you," and I almost lose it. I almost get up, get dressed, and walk out, but I'm tired. Maybe I can just ignore this whole night. Maybe we'll never talk about getting married again.

I'm almost asleep when she says, "You're still taking me to the airport tomorrow, right?"

"Yeah."

"I can't wait to tell my parents I'm engaged."

chapter fourteen

First Date

I drop Casey off at the airport at 5:30 P.M. I have to pick up Alyna for our date at 8:30. Casey kisses me on the cheek and says, "See you in a few days, fiancé."

"Right."

As I drive back to my apartment I hope her plane goes down or gets hijacked before she has a chance to tell her parents that we're engaged.

Back at home I prepare for my date by jerking off while watching a rerun of *90210*. I brush my teeth twice, take a dump, and then jerk off one more time in the shower just to make sure. I put on some clothes that I think are nice but not too nice, and wonder if Alyna will be wearing any underwear tonight. I wonder if she wears thong underwear. I imagine her ass in thong underwear. I jerk off again, then take a half shower in which I only scrub my dick and balls.

Alyna lives about three minutes away from my apartment in a university-owned off-campus apartment complex. I park my car and ring her apartment number on the call box of her building.

A girl says, "Hello."

"Hi, I'm here to pick Alyna up."

"She's still getting ready, but I'll buzz you in."

When I get to Alyna's door, I meet her roommate, Simone.

Simone is a hippie-type bitch who doesn't shave her armpits or wear shoes. Despite the fact that she's kind of fat, I wonder if there's any chance of getting both her and Alyna drunk and coaxing them into a threesome. I wonder if she would lick my balls while I fucked Alyna.

Simone says, "So what's your deal?"

"How's that?"

"What's your deal, man? What're you up to?"

"I'm just here to take Alyna out."

"Yeah, I know."

I sit down on their couch.

She says, "So where are you from?"

"Originally?"

"Yeah."

"I'm from Colorado. How about you?"

"Northern California. Santa Cruz."

"And you go to UCLA with Alyna?"

"Yeah."

"Have you known her long?"

"A year. You?"

"We actually just kind of met a week or so ago."

I'm suddenly repulsed at myself for trying to get this hippie bitch to like me, but the thought of her eating Alyna's pussy while I fuck her is enough for me to remain cordial.

She says, "Yeah, well, everybody meets everybody at one point in their relationship, you know, man?"

"Right."

Alyna comes out of some back room—maybe a bathroom, maybe a bedroom. She says, "Sorry. You ready to go?"

"Yeah. Nice to meet you, Simone."

I put my hand out to shake hers and she hugs me. She has mild body odor, but as her tits press against me I learn that they're full and kind of sloppy, which, surprisingly, doesn't repulse me.

Simone says, "You, too."

As we're walking out the door and I'm looking for a panty line on Alyna's ass in a pair of tight slack-type pants, she says, "Bye, Simone. Don't wait up." I can't see a panty line.

The ride to the restaurant is uneventful. She looks through the CDs I have in my car and we talk about our musical interests. As we pull into the restaurant parking lot she semi-leans over me to put a CD back in my sun visor CD carrying case and brushes me with her tit. It's a little smaller than I originally thought, but a rock-hard B cup nonetheless. I think about her straddling me as I lick and bite at her tits.

The restaurant is a French place called Le Petit Chateau in North Hollywood.

When we get inside, we start drinking wine and the conversation comes a little easier. We cover the basics—ages, interests, hometowns, and we skirt around the issue of previous relationships. I don't mention Casey.

A couple comes in and sits a few tables away from us. Alyna and I both notice them. The girl has a fucking amazing body, but her facial features are disproportionate in a way that makes me wonder if she has some kind of mild medical deformity.

She says, "Do you think they're on a first date, too?"

"I don't know."

"I bet they are."

"How can you tell?"

"It's all in the way the guy is treating her."

"And how's he treating her?"

"The same way you're treating me. He's trying to impress her. He's pulling her chair out, he's being really nice, and he's acting like he's really interested in whatever it is she's saying. He even unfolded the napkin and put it in his lap, just like you did when we sat down."

"What does the napkin have to do with it?"

"I bet you never do that when you just go out to eat with your guy friends or with somebody you're not trying to impress."

I think about the last several times I've gone out to eat with Casey. Alyna's right. She becomes immediately more attractive to me based on the fact that she seems smarter than Casey even though she's younger.

I say, "Maybe it is their first date."

She says, "Who do you think is having a better first date, us or them?"

"Definitely us."

"And why's that?"

"Because they're not looking at us wondering if it's our first date."

She smiles.

The guy from the couple gets up from the table and excuses himself.

Alyna says, "Where do you think he's going?"

"To the bathroom."

"What if he's going to call one of his friends to tell him how horrible the date is going and how he needs the friend to call him in the next ten minutes with some urgent emergency so he can get out of the date?"

"Do you have something like that planned to get out of this date?"

She laughs. "I might."

We get our food and start eating. She eats like a girl—taking small bites and covering her mouth with her hand. But the pasta she ordered makes her lips wet and all I can think about is her sucking my cock. I make it my goal to shoot a load down her throat before the night's over.

As we eat and talk some more we notice that the guy who left his first date earlier still hasn't come back. The hot-bodied bitch is sitting at the table by herself, getting visibly worried.

Alyna says, "I bet he snuck out the window or something. I feel so bad for that poor girl."

If the guy did sneak out the window, I admire him.

The front door opens and a guy in full knight armor walks in. Everybody in the place stops eating and watches the following first-date nightmare unfold.

The knight walks over to the table where the hot-bodied bitch is sitting alone and gets down on one knee. He flips up his visor and it's the guy who went to the bathroom twenty minutes ago. He proposes. She accepts. The whole place goes crazy. As Alyna stares in silence at the unfolding events, I can't tell if she's disgusted or on the verge of tears because this moment is so magical.

I want to know what's running through Alyna's head. It's probably something attaching far more meaning to this event than it deserves, especially since it happened on our first date. Casey would have thought the whole thing was a sign from God that we should get married.

To diffuse the situation I try to make a joke. "I guess they're having the better first date now."

She says, "That is so fucking stupid."

I can't tell if she's talking about the knight or about my joke.

She says, "Does that guy think he's being romantic?"

She's talking about the knight.

"It worked."

"I just think marriage is so stupid. Seriously, what we just saw basically defines all marriages—some guy makes an ass out of himself and the girl is too overwhelmed by it to think straight enough to say no."

I'm impressed. I say, "So you don't want to get married?"

"Look, I know this is kind of a big subject for a first date and everything, but no, I don't want to. I don't want to have kids either. What about you?"

"Same pretty much."

She smiles again.

As we finish eating, the newly engaged couple is visited by practically every woman in the place. They all tell the guy in the knight suit that it's the most romantic thing they've ever seen. Alyna just eats her pasta.

When we're done, I pay the tab and we leave.

Once we're in my car she says, "So what're we going to do now?"

"Whatever you want."

"I want to see where you live."

I wonder if I should fuck her doggie style on the first date.

As we walk through the front door of my apartment, I can feel my cell phone vibrating in my pocket. I know it's Casey, so I don't answer it.

I say, "Do you want something to drink?"

"No. I'm fine. How long have you lived here?"

She walks in and sits on my couch.

"A year or so."

I pour myself something to drink and then join her on the couch. Her pants are riding down in the back a little bit to give me a small shot of the top of her ass. She's wearing a thong, which contradicts my earlier assessment of no underwear at all.

I say, "So . . ."

She takes the cue, leans in, and kisses me. Her mouth is warm and wet and I can already feel it on my cock. I get a hard-on instantly.

She pulls back and looks at me.

She says, "I better get back home. I have some tests to study for this weekend."

I feel like I just hit a fucking brick wall going sixty and I'm flying through the windshield as I say, "What?"

"Yeah, I just have some things to do and I should really go home."

I'm too confused to be pissed off and I say, "Okay, if you have to go I'll give you a ride."

"That's okay, I can walk."

"It's late. I can drive you."

"No, really, it's fine."

She gets up off the couch and says, "I had a really good time tonight."

"Me too, so why are you leaving?"

"We just probably shouldn't see each other again."

"Why?"

"Listen, I should have never gone on a date with you in the first place. I have a boyfriend. We're having some problems right now, but he's still my boyfriend."

Holy shit. I want to tell her that I have a girlfriend, that it doesn't matter, that they don't have to know. Instead I say, "Oh . . ."

She kisses me on the cheek and says, "Seriously, thanks, I had a really good time and you're a really nice guy."

She turns to leave and I say, "Why did you go out with me in the first place?"

"I don't know. I'm sorry."

And she leaves. As she walks out the door, I wish I would have fucked her or at least felt one of her tits. I lie down on my couch and smell the spot she was sitting on. I jerk off to the thought of her sucking my cock. I shoot my load into a napkin that's been on my coffee table for a few days. I stare at the ceiling wondering if I could've fucked her if I had tried a little harder. I wonder if she'll fuck her boyfriend tonight. I wonder if he'll fuck her doggie style. I wonder if she'll think about me while he does.

I experience a surprising moment of genuine sadness as I realize that I might never see Alyna again, when my cell phone vibrates again and it's Casey calling from her parents' house in Nebraska. She asks me what I did tonight but doesn't let me answer before she tells me the good news that her parents were so excited when she announced our engagement that they're coming out to visit their future son-in-law in a few weeks.

She's still talking about something when I put the phone next to my head and fall asleep.

chapter fifteen

The Morning After

I wake up, take a shower, and realize I'm supposed to be eating lunch with my gay buddy Carlos in thirty minutes.

Forty-five minutes later, I walk into the Beverly Center California Pizza Kitchen to see Carlos sitting by himself and pissed off.

He says, "Where the fuck have you been, you little asshole?"

"I was tired. I forgot."

"You fucking forgot. You ungrateful piece of shit."

"Sorry."

"Well, now you have to buy my lunch because you're a fucker."

"Sure."

We get seated and look at the menus for no reason.

"Hey, see those two guys over there?" He looks in the direction of two guys in their late thirties sitting at a small table in the back. One of them is wearing a shirt with pink letters that read NAUGHTY BOY.

I say, "Yeah."

"The one with the brown hair has the smallest dick I've ever sucked. So what in the hell have you been up to besides making me wait to eat lunch when I'm fucking starving?"

"I had that date last night."

"Oh, right, that bitch you met in the video game store. And Casey doesn't know a thing?"

"Right."

"Well, how did it go? Did you at least get blown?"

"I thought it went pretty well until the end. She invited herself back to my house—"

"Wow, so you definitely got blown. You probably fucked her."

"I didn't get blown or fuck her. She kissed me and then said she had a boyfriend and had to leave."

"That little bitch. But seriously, that doesn't sound too bad. At least all she did was kiss you and at least all she had was a fucking boyfriend. I've been on my knees with cum dribbling out of my ass and down my chin and had some son of a bitch tell me he was married with kids. Try that one on for size."

"I just don't get why she even went out with me in the first place."

"Who the fuck knows? Women can be complete cunts. At least with guys you know they always go out with you to fuck you, plain and simple. That's why you went out with her, right?"

"Yeah. For the most part."

"What other part is there?"

"I don't know. None, I guess."

"Listen. It's better it ended up this way. I mean, Casey would've eventually found out about this thing if it had gone on for very long."

"I know."

"So count your blessings. You got to go on a date with a hot piece of ass and you still get to keep your girlfriend."

I almost wish I had answered the phone when Casey called the first time. I almost wish I had let her hear Alyna in the background. I wish I had the balls to call Casey right now and tell her I fucked some drunk bitch in the ass at her Groundlings party while posing as her teacher. I almost wish she wasn't my girlfriend.

The waiter comes to our table and we order the same things we always order and strike up the same conversations about the same things we always talk about for the rest of lunch. After an hour we leave.

When I get home, I put in the Tori Amos CD that I bought from Alyna and jerk off.

some chapter

Hobo

I'm walking out of Jerry's Famous Deli in Westwood when a semi-insane-looking hobo says, "Could you spare some change, brother?"

I have thirty-five cents in my pocket and I'm fully prepared to give it to him. I reach in my pocket, get the coins out, and begin the process of handing the money to the hobo when the following occurs.

Somebody says, "Don't do it."

I look over, and walking toward the hobo and myself is an Asian girl with fucking full-blown Down syndrome. She's wearing glasses and her tongue's kind of hanging out and she's waving her arms around like a maniac as she keeps saying, "Don't do it. Don't do it."

I pull the money back from the hobo, waiting for things to develop.

The retard says, "Mister, don't give him any money."

I say, "Okay."

She points her retarded finger at the hobo and says, "What's wrong with you? I make six dollars an hour. Why can't you get a job?"

The hobo is speechless. So am I. The retard's not.

She says, "You could get a job if you really wanted to, but you don't. You're lazy and I hate lazy people. You should not ask people for money that they've worked for. I would never give you money. I make six dollars an hour. I have a job. Why should I give you my money?"

I can't tell if the hobo is genuinely moved by the retard's rhetoric or by the poetic justice of this whole thing or what, but he stands up, says, "Shut your trap, I'm leaving," and takes off down the street. All the while the retard keeps yelling after him, "Get a job! I have a job!"

Once he's finally out of earshot the retard turns to me and says, "You should never give them your money. They are lazy. I hate them." Then she turns around and trudges off down the street. I hope she's on her way to deliver some more motivational speeches to hobos.

When I get home I wonder what retards are like when they fuck—if they're crazy, or if they go limp. I wonder if they're any good at sucking dick and I decide I would fuck a retard if given the opportunity so I could answer these questions.

chapter sixteen

Casey's Homecoming

I'm at the airport to pick up Casey. As I'm waiting by the baggage claim I see a guy in a brown jacket holding some flowers that he probably bought at the airport for his girlfriend. I know Casey would like me to be waiting for her with flowers. I see the little guy selling the flowers. I also see an average-looking bitch standing across from me. We exchange a glance. Casey's plane lands in ten minutes. I wonder if the average-looking bitch would accept a no-strings-attached offer to fuck in the bathroom. I wonder who she's here to pick up. Probably her boyfriend, who probably bought flowers for her at whatever airport he's coming from. Casey's been gone for two days, in which time I haven't fucked. I decide to buy her flowers.

Fifteen minutes later Casey wanders out into the baggage claim area like a lost little kid along with all the other people who were on her flight. The guy in the brown jacket gives his flowers to a girl who doesn't look that much different from the average-looking bitch. She kisses him. The average-looking bitch gets flowers from a guy who doesn't look that much different from the guy in the brown jacket. She kisses him. I give my flowers to Casey. She hugs me and kisses me and says, "Oh, thank you. You're so sweet."

As she's hugging me I feel her tits through her shirt. I whisper in her ear, "Let's get your bags and go straight to your house and fuck."

She says, "I can't believe we're engaged. Can you?"

I don't know if I had convinced myself that it was all a bad dream or if I had forced the memory of three nights ago so far down that I couldn't remember it, but we're engaged. Casey thinks we're engaged and she told her parents that we're engaged and now I'm giving her flowers in an airport. We're fucking engaged.

She says, "When I told my mom she started crying."

I can't say anything. I let go of her and start walking over to the baggage carousel. She follows me, still talking.

"My dad was like, 'Well, I guess we can expect another grandchild pretty soon.'"

I look around the baggage claim, kind of frantic. I need to find something that makes me think I shouldn't run out and throw myself in front of the first SuperShuttle I see. I see a semi-hot bitch with a great ass and a pretty good cocksucking mouth. I tell myself that I may have a very slim chance of ever fucking a girl like that, but if I'm dead I'll have no chance. I keep walking toward the baggage carousel. Casey keeps talking.

"At first I thought my dad was nuts, but I guess he's kind of right, you know? I mean, after you get married, it's like kids usually come pretty soon after. Do you want to have a boy or a girl first?"

I can feel the cold sweat dripping down the middle of my back into my ass crack. I wonder if Casey stopped taking the pill after the conversation with her dad. Maybe I should insist that we start using rubbers. Maybe I should only let her suck my dick. Casey keeps talking.

The first few bags come out of the baggage chute. They hit the carousel and start their crawl around it. The bitch who saved me from committing suicide comes over and stands right next to me. I stare at her ass. Casey keeps talking.

"You know, I think we should move in together before we get married. Maybe we could get a little dog, too. I don't know, though. The cats might not like having a dog. I guess the dog could be a strictly outside dog if we could get a place with a yard—somewhere in the Valley." I fucking despise the Valley.

As I'm staring at this girl's ass I notice she's trying to get a bag that slid past her and is now right in front of me. I reach down and get it. She brushes my arm with her hand as I lift it off the carousel. She looks up at me and smiles. She says, "Thanks," pops out the little handle, and shakes her ass out the door toward the waiting taxis. Casey keeps talking.

The rest of what she says is inaudible to me. Whatever she says becomes a high-pitched ringing in my ears. I grab her bag when I see it and we leave.

That night she says she loves me a few dozen times, she coaxes me into taking a bubble bath with her, she wears some lingerie she hasn't worn since Valentine's Day when I bought it for her, she snuggles up next to me, we don't fuck, and I fall asleep wondering if our daughters would be cursed with Casey's fat ass.

chapter seventeen

Chance Encounter

Casey and I have been engaged for a few weeks now. I haven't told any of my friends or family members. Casey has told all of hers multiple times. I'm listening to one of them congratulate Casey in the food court of the Beverly Center.

Her friend says, "Oh, I'm so happy for you guys."

Casey says, "Thanks. We're really excited. We're thinking about getting a place together."

Her friend says, "Oh my god, that is so fun. When Ronny and I got our place it was like the best day of my life, except for the wedding, of course." Then she pukes out a laugh.

Casey says, "Yeah. I can't wait."

Her friend says, "When's the big date?"

Casey says, "We really haven't picked one out yet. Probably sometime in the summer."

Her friend says, "You still have my address and everything to send an invite, right?"

Casey says, "Of course."

Her friend says, "Great," then she fake-whispers this next bit to Casey: "And don't forget to let me know about the bachelorette party."

Casey fake-whispers back, "I won't."

They hug and Casey says, "And don't be a stranger, let's get lunch sometime."

Her friend says, "Okay, I'll give you a call. You kids behave." Then she heads toward the escalators.

Casey says, "Have we ever come to the Beverly Center and not run into someone we know? Seriously, it's like everyone in town comes here on the weekends."

I start walking toward the Orange Julius/Dairy Queen without hearing what she just said. I remember in seventh grade home-ec class, Mrs. Baker taught us how to make Orange Julius with vanilla extract, orange juice, sugar, and ice. Mrs. Baker wasn't particularly attractive but I would have fucked her.

I buy a chocolate-dipped cone and Casey gets a small Julius. As we leave the counter I literally bump into Alyna, who is walking by with her arm around some asshole. A conversation is unavoidable and I'm sure it's going to lead to the discovery of our date by both of our significant others. But I'm more worried about Alyna finding out I have a girlfriend.

Alyna says, "Oh, hey. How are you?"

"I'm fine, you?"

"Pretty good."

"This is my boyfriend, Duane."

I fucking shake his hand. Casey gets tired of not being introduced and says, "I'm his fiancée, Casey. Nice to meet you guys."

Alyna shakes Casey's hand and says, "Hi, I'm Alyna." I can tell Alyna's surprised. I feel worse than I should for never telling her about Casey. Even though I have no chance with her, for some reason I still don't want her to be mad at me.

Casey is jealous immediately. She says, "So how do you two know each other?"

I kind of want to let it all out, expose the truth, see what happens. Alyna answers before I can say anything. She says, "I had a flat tire over in Westwood and your husband-to-be here helped me change it."

Holy shit. This is the most insane lie I've ever heard in my life. There's no way either of our respective counterparts will swallow it.

Casey says, "I didn't know you knew how to change a tire."

I say, "Well, I do."

Casey says, "Huh. I'll have to remember that," then she laughs.

Duane also laughs for some reason.

Alyna says, "Well, you guys take it easy. We have some shopping to get to."

I say, "Yeah. You, too."

As they walk away, Alyna says, "It was good to see you again."

I say, "Yeah. You, too."

I try to convince myself that this was just a strange coincidence, that there was no greater purpose behind running into Alyna, that she isn't thinking about me as she walks through the Beverly Center with Duane.

Casey says, "You never told me you helped somebody change their tire. That's a good story, why didn't you tell me about that?"

"I don't know."

"Do you want to go look at invitations or rings?"

I want to turn around, chase after Alyna, and never have to hear Casey's voice again. I say, "You pick."

some chapter

Internet Personals

After downloading some double-dong lesbian pornography I check my e-mail. In my inbox is a message from Caligurrl669 with the following as a subject heading: "Saw you on match.com and thought you looked cute."

Despite having numerous profiles on different Internet personals sites for almost a year, this is the first e-mail response I've ever received. I open it.

Caligurrl669 tells me that she thinks I look like Eric Stoltz, who is one of her favorite actors. She recently moved to Los Angeles from Ohio to become an actress. She loves the Cure and the Smiths. She doesn't consider herself religious, but she is very spiritual. She has a dog and wants to know if I like animals. The last guy she dated was really into pro wrestling. She wasn't. She wants to know if I'm really into pro wrestling. She signs the e-mail with a smiley face and a link to her profile. I check the link.

Caligurrl669 is a little chubbier than I imagined from her e-mail, but not fat. Her tits are a little smaller than I imagined, but not bad. Her face is acceptable.

I wonder if Caligurrl669 sucks dick on the first date. I wonder if shes likes anal sex. I wonder if Caligurrl669 is actually a guy trying to lure me into showing up somewhere so he can beat the shit out of me and take whatever cash I brought.

I respond with the following message:

> Caligurrl669—
> I only set up dates with girls who send me nude photos of themselves accompanied by detailed descriptions of how they perform fellatio. To further pique my interest you might want to do something in the photos that lets me know you have a unique talent, you know, something to separate you from the crowd. I look forward to your response.

Caligurrl669 probably won't ever write me again and that doesn't bother me. But then again, she might.

chapter eighteen

Casey's Parents

Over the course of our relationship, Casey's parents have come to Los Angeles to visit her several times. I've eaten dinner with them more than once and have been forced to endure multiple trips to the mall with them and Casey to look for clothes. As much as I hated all of that, the prospect of spending the next two days with them as their future son-in-law is on a different level of agony. But somehow the impending doom of my life ending in marriage to Casey is less threatening than the more immediate disaster that would result from breaking up with her now.

We're in my car on the way to LAX to pick her parents up. Casey says, "Remember, you can't curse around my mom. She'll think you're a bad influence and that our marriage will be bad. And offer to pay for things. You'll never have to, but if you offer to pay for things my dad will think you're a provider and that's good. And don't bring up France with my dad. He'll go crazy and won't stop talking for an hour. And if my mom asks you where you think we're going to live, just tell her that it's still up in the air and it really depends on where we can find the best place. And if they ask you about a wedding date, tell them a.s.a.p. And if either of them ask you about when we're going to have kids, just say as soon as we get settled we're going to start trying. Wait, maybe don't say anything about trying because they'll think about us having sex and I don't want my parents thinking about that. Just say as soon as we're settled."

When we exit the 405, there's a hobo with a sign that reads HOMELESS, HUNGRY, AND HANDSOME—ANYTHING WILL HELP at the first stoplight. I like his sign so I roll down my window. He walks in between a few cars also stopped at the red light and holds out his hand. I reach in my pocket and realize I only have a five-dollar bill. I don't really want to give him five dollars, but I already rolled down my window and now he's standing at it. I give him the five-dollar bill. He thanks me, the light turns green, and we keep driving. Despite the satisfaction I genuinely get from giving hobos money, I gave this guy money specifically to get the following reaction from Casey:

"Why do you give them money? It's so stupid. They just spend it on drugs and booze."

There's something about her hating the fact that I give hobos money that makes me happy.

We park at LAX and go into the baggage claim area to wait for Casey's mom and dad to come out. She says, "God, isn't this exciting. I mean, I know you've met them before and everything, but you've never actually met them as your future in-laws. Seriously, aren't you excited?"

I think she's asking a rhetorical question so I don't answer.

She says, "Well, aren't you?"

"Yeah."

Some people start coming out of a door toward the baggage claim.

Casey says, "Do you think that's their flight?"

I think I want to walk back to my car and drive back to my apartment and play World of Warcraft. I think I don't want to spend the next two days being dragged around L.A. looking at clothes I couldn't care less about and eating food when I'm not hungry. I think I don't want to do this anymore.

Her mom and dad walk through the door and spot us. Her mom half jogs over to Casey with a big smile on her face, while her dad is left to drag both of their carry-on bags behind him.

Her mom says, "Oh, congratulations, you two. I just knew Casey would get married one day. I just knew it. My little girl. And you," she says to me, "come here."

She gives me a big hug and says, "It's about time, huh? We were starting to wonder about you."

For an older woman Casey's mom has a noticeably nice ass. I wonder if Casey's will slim down if I stay with her until she's in her fifties.

Casey's dad finally manages to make it over to the group. He says, "So, my little girl's getting hitched?" He gives her a hug, then turns to me and says, "And I'm going to have a new son." He shakes my hand in a weird kind of overexcited way.

Casey's mom says, "So we thought we could go eat a little lunch when we get out of here and then you guys can drop us off at our hotel for a few hours so we can rest for a bit, and then you can come back and pick us up and we can go shopping, or I figured that you guys would probably start looking for a place to live together . . . we could come with you. That would be so much fun. How does that sound?"

Casey says, "That's exactly the way I had it planned, too."

If I had a cyanide pill I would probably eat it.

Casey's dad says, "Great. We just have a few bags."

We wait at the baggage carousel for a few bags, which turns out to be five.

When we get in my car and I start it, I become immediately aware that Casey forgot to take my Snoop Dogg CD out and Casey's parents are treated to the following pro-marriage rhetoric:

You talk too much
Ho get up out my face unless you tryin' to fuck
'Cause on the real a nigga kinda drunk

Casey turns the music off before Snoop can say anything else. Everyone in the car heard it and no one's saying anything. I put the car in reverse and pull out of my parking spot. No one's saying anything. I start driving to the parking structure exit. No one's saying anything. I pull up to the booth, grab my ticket off the dashboard, and roll down my window. Casey's dad says, "I just can't get over how nice the weather here is."

We pull up to the booth and I give my ticket to a little Asian guy. The meter flashes $3.00. The little Asian guy hammers it home by saying, "Three dollars, please."

I realize I gave my last five dollars to the hobo on the way into the airport. Casey said her parents would never let me pay for anything, I just had to make the offer. I say, "I got it." I reach in my pocket to make the offer seem real. I'm feeling around inside my empty pocket when I hear Casey's parents say nothing.

I don't know if they're pissed at me for Snoop Dogg or if this is the one time they're actually making me pay for something as some kind of test. In either case I have no way of paying the three dollars. The little Asian guy says again with exactly the same inflection, "Three dollars, please."

Casey's getting nervous next to me. She turns back and smiles to her parents. She says, "How was your flight?" She's trying to stall them, but it's not working. I can see her mom's face in my rearview mirror. She's getting anxious. Her dad looks disappointed. Deep down I don't really care about any of it. And I'm kind of happy when I say, "That's funny, I don't seem to have any money on me. I guess I just gave my last five dollars to that homeless guy."

Casey's mom reaches for her purse and says, "Why do you give them money? They only spend it on drugs and drink." Then she adds,

"I think I have three dollars." She's almost disgusted when she hands me the bills.

I say, "Thanks, sorry about that. Dinner's on me tonight."

Casey's dad says, "Don't be silly. It's only three dollars." But I can tell he's pissed, too. It's more than just three dollars to him. It's the guy who's about to marry his little girl not being able to get out of a parking lot. I hope it keeps him awake at night. I hope I'm the secretly hated fiancé, the one they complain about to their friends at the country club, the one who always gets shitty presents at family Christmas parties, the one who ruins their perfect family.

As we pull out of the parking structure, Casey says, "So where do you guys want to eat?"

I know her dad is thinking that now I can't even offer to pay for lunch because everyone knows I have no money. I think I might offer anyway. Her dad says, "Somewhere with steak."

Her mom says, "You already had your steak for the week."

He says, "We're on vacation."

She says, "That doesn't matter. You're not having another steak. Casey, you pick."

Casey says, "Okay, I know a good place. Daddy, there's no steak but I think you'll like it."

He says, "Do they have beer?"

Casey's mom says, "You can't have any more beer this week either. Are you just trying to kill yourself right before your daughter's wedding? Is that what you want?"

He says, "It's my vacation."

She says, "That doesn't matter. Your heart doesn't go on vacation and neither does your high blood pressure."

They keep arguing as we drive down the road to one of Casey's favorite lunch places, the Daily Grill. I wonder if they still fuck or when the last time was that she sucked his cock.

chapter nineteen

Apartment Hunting

We've been in the Valley, Toluca Lake, for four hours looking at apartments with Casey's parents and a woman from a rental agency that Casey called, who seems to be in her mid-thirties with great tits. I fucking despise the Valley. I'm standing in the living room of the third place we've looked at today. Casey, her mom, and the rental agency lady are in the bedroom. Her dad's standing with me.

He says, "So how'd you propose to my little girl?"

I try to remember exactly how we became engaged. I can't. I only vaguely think Casey invited me over to fuck and then somehow we were engaged without fucking.

I say, "I got down on one knee."

He says, "I figured you for a one-knee man. That's how I popped the question to her mother, too. One knee's the best way to go. It's not too creative, but it gets the job done and it's classy. Things like that are important moments in a woman's life and they should be classy." He pats me on the back, then says, "You know, Casey's sister just had a baby. Do you think you guys'll have kids pretty soon after you're married?"

I can't remember what Casey told me I was supposed to say but I think it was something like, "Yeah."

He says, "That's great. That's really the only way to do it. Start your family early, then when you get to be my age you have some time for yourself. Not that raising kids is all bad or anything, but trust me, when you hit forty-five you can barely stand your wife, let alone kids running around the house. But don't get me wrong, marriage is a wonderful thing."

Casey, her mom, and the rental agency woman walk in from the other room. Casey's mom is pointing at the walls, saying, "You could do some amazing things in here. There's so much light. Really, this would make a great family area. And that little half bedroom would be perfect for the baby. This place is absolutely perfect."

The realtor says, "It really is perfect for married couples just starting out. The last tenants were a married couple and they were here for two and a half years, and now that they have their third baby on the way and a little more money in their pockets, they're going to buy their first house."

Casey says, "I can't wait till we can buy our first house together." Then she hugs me. I wonder if the rental agency woman would do a three-way with me and Casey, or if she'd just suck my cock if I stopped by her office one day.

Casey's dad says, "Well, do you guys think this is the one?"

Casey says, "I really like it."

Her dad says, "Then you guys should get the ball rolling—no time like the present."

Casey says, "I guess you're right. What do we need to fill out?"

The rental agency woman says, "Well, we can start getting the paperwork in order, but it really depends on when you'd want to move in. The current tenants officially move out in a couple of months. I don't know when the big wedding date is for you guys and how that fits into your plans, but that's the soonest they could be out."

Casey's mom says, "I can't believe we never even asked when you're getting married."

Casey says, "Well, we wanted to have some time to plan it out and everything, but if we need to be ready to move, I guess we could move things up."

Casey's mom says, "I'll help you plan everything. It'll go like clockwork. You can still have a beautiful wedding even in a few months."

Casey says, "Would you really help me plan it, Mom?"

Her mom says, "Of course. I know exactly how everything should be."

Everything else either one of them says becomes a high-pitched ringing in my ears. I think about Alyna and wonder what would have happened if I hadn't gone over to Casey's house that night to fuck.

Later as we're eating dinner to celebrate the paperwork being started on our new apartment, I look at Casey's dad and try to picture myself at his age, visiting my daughter who's forced some guy into a marriage he doesn't want. I wonder if Casey's dad really wanted to marry her mom. I wonder if there was a girl like Alyna for him. I wonder how many times a day he jerks off. I wonder if I'll still jerk off when I'm his age.

When we're finished with dinner I offer to pay and her parents let me.

some chapter

Blood Cock

When Casey has her period she refuses to suck my dick and she's very uncomfortable with fucking. I usually have to coax her into it by promising to buy her dinner at one of her favorite restaurants. As I'm fucking her on this particular occasion I've only had to promise to take her for ice cream.

She's lying on a towel so the blood that runs down her ass crack doesn't get on the sheets. As I fuck her I look down at her face and she's completely uninterested. I decide to make sure she gets off just to prove to myself I can do it at will. I slow down my pace a little and reach down with one hand to play with her clit. This seems to be working at least on a rudimentary level.

I lean down and whisper in her ear, "I love you so much. I can't wait until we can make love in our own house."

She starts moaning.

I kiss her slowly on the lips and take the hand I was using on her clit and touch her face. After the kiss I pull back and look into her eyes, ignoring the bloody smear I left on her cheek. I say, "I can't wait to spend the rest of my life with you."

She moans louder. She reaches around and grabs me by the ass, pulling me toward her.

I go back to stroking her clit and say, "I love you more than anything."

She cums like a ton of bricks so I stop holding back and blow my load with three deep, hard thrusts.

When I pull out I make sure to hang my cock over her stomach to let some of the blood and semen drip off my dick onto her stomach, knowing this will disgust her.

As I'm getting up to go to the bathroom, she says, "That was better than I thought it was going to be."

We take a shower together to clean up. I watch the blood and semen run down her legs and into the shower drain. She cleans her cunt but doesn't wash her face, leaving the smudge of blood so it's still there when we leave a few minutes later to get her ice cream.

chapter twenty

Bon Voyage

I'm at the airport with Casey and her parents eating chicken strips in a Chili's Too. I've had to shit since I woke up, but Casey told me there wasn't enough time to drop a deuce because her parents had to be at the airport. Casey's mom says, "I'll be out here again next weekend to help you start planning for the big day."

I wish I would have taken that shit.

Casey says, "Are you coming back, Daddy?"

He says, "Not if you want me to pay for it. I have to work."

Casey's mom says, "So it'll just be me. And I'll stay as long as it takes to get everything together."

I don't particularly dislike Casey's mom, but the prospect of her staying "as long as it takes to get everything together" makes the impending shit lurch in my intestines and want to come out.

Casey tries to coax the turd out a little more by saying, "Mom, if you don't want to hassle with a hotel while you're out here, you can always just stay with me."

I immediately picture Casey refusing to suck my cock or fuck me because her mom's in her apartment. I chew my chicken strip hard enough to grind my teeth down to nubs.

Casey's dad says, "That wouldn't be a bad idea except for your mom's back. You know she wouldn't be able to sleep on your futon."

Casey saves the day with, "Well, I could sleep on it while you're out here and you could have the bed."

My intestines are at full boil. I say, "Excuse me, I have to go to the bathroom."

As I leave the table kind of abruptly I can tell Casey's mom is somehow offended that I'm exiting while they talk about obviously important matters. When I stand up a silent fart leaks out and I try to point my ass slightly in the direction of Casey's mom so there's a possibility that she'll be blamed for it.

After I clean off the toilet seat in the Chili's Too bathroom and apply three toilet seat covers, I rip my pants down and open the floodgates as a torrent of liquid shit flies out of my ass in a way that makes me think I might have possibly shit some vital organ into the water below. And then I feel fine.

I sit on the crapper for another five or six minutes before wiping, just feeling lighter, better. When I come back out, all of our food has already been cleared away and Casey's dad is signing his credit card bill. I thank him for lunch in a mandatory attempt at politeness.

We walk with her parents to the security check. Her mom hugs me and her dad shakes my hand just before they walk through the metal detectors and disappear around a corner to go to their flight.

As I drive back to Casey's place with her in the passenger seat, I reach over and start unbuttoning her pants with one hand, trying to get her in the mood so once we do get to her apartment we can get right to fucking. As I get to the second button she stops me and holds my hand.

We drive down the road in complete silence for a few miles listening to 50 Cent. As soon as he tells us that he's into having sex, he ain't into making love, Casey turns the volume down and begins telling me the following information: "I love you so much. We're going to have the best life together. I can't wait." Every word she says makes me feel a little more like faking a stroke and pretending to lose all memory of who I was, but it's not until she looks me in the eye and says in all seriousness, "You're my soul mate," that I realize I am not going to marry her.

chapter twenty-one

Be the King

Todd and I are at a bar in Westwood. Next to us is a table full of seven Asian bitches playing some kind of card game. Three of them are extremely hot and the rest are definitely worth fucking or at least getting head from.

Todd says, "So what's the deal now, you're getting married to Casey?"

"No. I'm not."

"But you just said her mom is coming back here to start planning the wedding in a few days, dude."

"Right."

"So when are you planning on not marrying her?"

"I don't know."

"Dude, do you think those Asian sluts would let us play with them?"

"I don't know."

"Dude, I'm gonna ask 'em."

And he does. The hottest one of them all appears to be the only one who speaks English and answers for the whole group when she says, "If you want play with, you and friend can play with."

Todd and I sit down at their table and listen to the following explanation of a new card game we've never heard of. "Okay, we play Be the King. It go like this. We have nine person to play so there will be cards one, two, three, four, five, six, seven, eight, and then king."

She starts pulling out the ace through eight of clubs and a king.

"Okay, now I deal."

She gives everybody at the table a card.

"Okay, now you look at card, but no show to us."

Todd and I look at our cards. I have the three of clubs.

"Okay, now who has king?"

One of the Asian girls sitting next to Todd goes fucking crazy, tosses her king into the middle of the table, and starts screaming, "I king, I king!"

The one who speaks English calms her down, "Okay, okay, okay. Now that she king, she tell us what to do."

I'm semi-drunk by this point and completely confused until the "king" says something of which I understand the following, "Okay, four—seven—"

The girl who speaks English explains to us that her friend, the king, has told whoever has the four and whoever has the seven to kiss for thirty seconds. And the game has just become infinitely more interesting and corroborates a long-held theory of mine that there are only two kinds of Asian girls—nymphomaniacs and corpses.

We all reveal our cards and it turns out that two of the really hot girls are four and seven. They kiss each other in this innocent giddy way that gives me a hard-on immediately. Todd and I agree to somehow let each other know which cards we pull.

In the next round I pull the king and Todd tips the corner of his card my way to show me he has the five. I say, "Okay, everyone except the king, kiss number five." Our friend, whose American name we've learned is Danni, translates it to her pals. They do a gang kiss on Todd, sometimes kissing each other.

The next round I pull a four and Todd shows me via a less stealthy and progressively drunker upturn of the corner of his card that he's drawn the eight. One of the semi-attractive Asian girls has drawn the king. She commands one of the girls to take another girl's head and pretend to smash it into a wall. Then the girl whose head was pretend-smashed into the wall has to scream and pretend her head really was smashed into the wall. Despite the fact that this act is in no way sexual, it is highly entertaining.

The longer we play, the more Todd and I try to turn Be the King into an orgy of Asian bitches to which we've somehow become privy, but there's something about these girls that won't allow us to succeed. They're naive and it seems like they're probably virgins and all of them find just as much excitement in pretending to beat each other up as they do in kissing each other.

The next time I get the king, I decide to see how far I can take it. I know Todd has a three, so I say, "Number four and number five have to suck the king's dick."

Danni says, "What is dick?"

I say, "Penis."

She says, "What is penis?"

I point to my crotch.

She says, "Oh," and giggles, then translates it for all of her buddies. They all giggle and start looking down at the ground. Four and Five start talking to Danni.

She says, "They say they no want to do that."

"But I'm the king."

"If they no want to, they no have to."

"Then what's the point of being the king?"

"To have fun and do funny thing."

"A blow job is a funny thing, Danni."

They all start talking to each other for about a minute. Todd and I just drink our beers. I look around the bar and notice that a group of people has kind of surrounded our table and has been watching us play this game for a while. Finally the Asian bitches come to a consensus.

Danni says, "We all go now."

Todd says, "No, you don't have to go, dude. We can let you be the king and slap each other around or whatever you guys want to do. Don't go."

Danni says, "We need to sleep for tests. It nice meeting you."

With that, Danni and her gang of Asian girls leave the table and the bar, leaving Todd to dispense the following accusation, "You made them leave, you fucker. If you hadn't scared them off by commanding them to give you a blow job, we could have—"

I say, "What, gotten blow jobs?"

Todd laughs. We discuss the nature of the game and how bizarre the Asian girls were before the conversation returns to Casey.

Todd says, "Seriously, dude, what's so bad about marrying her? Free house, she has rich parents—all that shit sounds good to me."

"Yeah, I guess."

"Then you should do it. I mean, fuck, dude, free fucking house. She ain't bad lookin'—that's pretty sweet."

"Yeah." No.

Later that night, after I've gone home, I lie awake staring at the ceiling and jerking off to thoughts of fucking the Asian girls we played Be the King with, which somehow reminds me of the first time I fucked my high school girlfriend, Katy. I remember the first time I shot a load down her throat when I shoot a load all over my own hand and the postejaculatory calm washes over me. For the first time in a while, Casey and my life's ruin is the furthest thing from my mind.

I wipe the semen off my hand and my dick with a towel that was lying on my floor and stay awake for a few more minutes wondering if I should have asked the Asian bitches to have anal sex with me, if somehow that would have offended them less. I also wonder if some of them were willing to suck my dick and Danni or one of the other bitches convinced them to leave. I wish Casey was Asian. I wish I hadn't thought about Casey.

some chapter

Little Kids

I'm eating a cheeseburger at Topz on Melrose. This semi-old-looking bitch is sitting a few tables away from me with a little girl who's probably about two or three years old. Across the room there's another bitch with a little boy who's probably about the same age.

The little boy keeps staring at the little girl and touching his cock. I wonder if he's actually thinking about fucking her or if he's getting a boner and doesn't know what it is or if he's just pawing at his dick because that's what little kids do. I myself don't think I ever thought about fucking when I was two, but I don't really remember.

As I keep looking at these little kids and wondering if they're thinking about fucking each other, I can't help thinking that at some point in each of these two-year-old kids' lives, they're going to be fucking somebody. That two-year-old girl whose mom dressed her up in a little pink dress to take her to Topz after Sunday church is going to suck cock, take it up the ass, have load after load of semen shot in her face, and eventually have another little girl who's eventually going to do all the same shit. And that little two-year-old boy whose mom dressed him in his Spider-Man T-shirt to take him to eat lunch after his favorite morning cartoons is going to fuck a girl, eat pussy, get twat hairs stuck in his throat, get his dick sucked, and someday have kids who will do all the same shit.

I wonder if either of the kids' parents have thought about any of this. I wonder if I'll have kids. If I do have kids I wonder if I'll look at them and think about them eventually fucking. I wonder if my parents ever thought about me fucking. I wonder if my parents are still fucking.

chapter twenty-two

Hi, Mom

I spend the night at Casey's apartment because we have to meet her mom at the airport the following morning and Casey wants me to drive. I assume that we'll fuck because this is the last night we have before her mom is in town and possibly in Casey's house for an indefinite amount of time. At 11:43 P.M. Casey's snoring makes me realize I shouldn't have assumed anything.

I'm unable to sleep, and my restless libido starts turning into rage. I lay awake staring at the ceiling listening to the sound of Casey's nose whistling in between her snorting gasps for air. I have to fuck. I nudge her a couple of times.

"Casey, Casey."

She wakes up. "What? I was asleep."

"Let's make love."

"My mom's coming tomorrow morning. We have to get to sleep."

"But don't you want to make love one more time before your mom gets here?"

"Why?"

She doesn't understand, or maybe she just doesn't care that once her mom is in town the frequency with which we have sex will be cut in half, or probably even worse. I say, "Because I love you."

"I love you, too. But I'm tired and I don't want to be even more tired when my mom gets here."

She kisses me on the cheek and rolls over, turning her fat ass toward me. She says, "Good night."

I can't take it. I get out of her bed.

She says, "Where are you going?"

"I have to go to the bathroom."

She goes back to sleep never knowing that I walk into the bathroom and jerk off into a bottle of special color treatment shampoo that she bought because it was featured on an Oprah show as one of Oprah's favorite things. As I jerk off, I think about kissing Alyna and fantasize about fucking her. For a split second, just before I cum, I entertain the thought of leaving Casey's apartment and driving to Alyna's to see if she'd be up for going to get coffee, but then I blow my load and I calm down enough to wipe off the top of the bottle, screw the lid back on, put it back in Casey's shower, and crawl back into bed with her.

I dream about nothing.

I wake up the next morning to an already awake and chipper Casey saying, "Come on, sleepyhead, it's time to take a shower and get ready to go pick up my mom."

We take a shower together. She uses her special color treatment shampoo. I use the Pert that's been in her shower as long as I've known her—probably left there by a previous boyfriend. Seeing her massage nine parts shampoo and one part semen into a thick lather on her head is more satisfying than any sex the night before could have been.

In the car on the way to the airport Casey turns off the volume on my stereo, which was playing "Xxplosive" from Dr. Dre's *Chronic 2001*. She says, "You know you can't listen to that when my mom gets in the car. She'd be completely offended. I mean, I'm actually kind of offended, too. But I guess because I'm younger and like I've grown up with rap music, I can at least deal with the way they talk about women. But my mom would not be okay with it."

I let her turn off my music without any rebuttal.

Then she says, "I'm sorry about last night, you know, not wanting to make love, but I think that other things are just a little more important right now. I mean we're about to start planning our wedding. That's like a day that we'll remember for the rest of our lives."

She keeps talking about things as I stare down the road trying to imagine what the couple in the car in front of us is talking about. I can see the silhouette of the woman in the passenger's seat. She's kind of flailing her arms around and every once in a while pointing at the guy driving, who's completely motionless, staring straight ahead and probably looking at the car in front of him wondering what the woman in that car's passenger seat is saying to the guy driving.

As I pull into a parking space in structure #4 at LAX I realize Casey is still talking about something. I hear, ". . . take us to breakfast at the Griddle, which I know you don't like, but can you just eat something and pretend to like it for me? I mean, she is going to be your mother-in-law in a few months. It would be nice if you could just pretend that you can eat breakfast with her at her favorite place in L.A. and not make a big deal about it."

I want her to shut up. I say, "Okay." It doesn't work.

"And don't be rude and order something that's not on the menu. The last time we went there, you asked the guy if they could make you a plate of scrambled eggs with nothing else in it. How embarrassing. If you want scrambled eggs, just get an omelet or something and cut it up."

When we get in the terminal we find out her mom's flight is fifteen minutes late, which Casey insists is a perfect amount of time to go look in the gift shop. I flip through an issue of *Hustler* that someone has already taken out of the plastic and left on the rack. Casey flips through Oprah's latest issue until she sees me staring at a pair of huge tits and a shaved pussy.

In a forced whisper she says, "Put that down."

I pretend not to hear her and flip the page to see another bitch spreading her friend's cunt open in preparation to lick it.

Casey walks over to me and closes the magazine while I'm still holding it. A naked bitch on the cover grabbing her own tits is still plainly visible to anyone walking by. Casey says, "How could you be looking at that right now?"

"It was the most interesting thing on the stand."

"My mother's going to be here in"—she checks her watch—"ten minutes. You can't be looking at that."

"You were the one who wanted to come look in the gift shop."

"Just put it back."

Even though I decide it's not worth getting into a fight over and put the *Hustler* back, the angry dissatisfaction I felt last night hits me tenfold and the thought of spending another second with Casey without fucking her makes me want to kill somebody.

She puts her magazine back and I walk with her to the baggage claim area, where we're supposed to meet her mom. I see at least a dozen other guys standing with girls. I wonder how many of them fucked their girlfriends last night.

Ten more minutes or so pass and Casey tries to explain to me how important it is to choose just the right kind of wedding invitation. She says that even though I won't be involved in the process of choosing the invitations, it's important for me to understand why she and her mother end up choosing whichever invitations they choose. She further explains that she wants something new and hip, but still traditional enough that her grandparents won't think she's moved to Hollywood and gone crazy. Then she laughs.

I try to imagine what she'd look like thirty pounds lighter. I can't. Her mom finally comes down an escalator and out to meet us.

She says, "Give me a hug, Casey. Long time no see." Then she laughs.

Casey says, "So did you get a hotel or did you decide to stay at my place?"

"I thought I'd stay at your apartment tonight so we can talk about a game plan."

"That's a great idea."

"So are you guys ready to go get some breakfast?"

We wait for her bags and drive to the Griddle, one of my least favorite places to eat.

chapter twenty-three

The Griddle

I figure Casey won't be fucking me for at least a few days anyway, so I order the plate of scrambled eggs with nothing else in it that Casey has forbidden me to get. Casey and her mom both pretend not to hear me when I ask the guy if they can make it for me. Even though I've already ordered it, before the guy leaves our table I throw in the following knife twist for good measure, "Now you're sure there'll be nothing else in the eggs?"

He says, "No. It'll just be eggs. I mean, it's not on the menu, but we can make it for you."

"Thanks."

Then he leaves. Casey's mom can't stand that I ordered a plate of scrambled eggs with nothing else in it. She doesn't even look at me as she says, "Do you always order things that aren't on the menu?"

I say, "Sometimes. Not always."

She still can't deal with it. She says, "It's just kind of strange. They have a whole variety of items that contain scrambled eggs. I just don't know why any one of those dishes isn't good enough."

And it's right then that I know I never want to see this woman again. I never want to hear her voice and I never want to placate her just to make Casey happy and I never want to deal with her in any way.

The waiter comes back with our drinks just as Casey's mom is getting fired up about my eggs. She calms down. As he leaves, she changes the topic of conversation entirely with, "Casey, your father wanted me to tell you that he's really sorry he couldn't come out and he wishes he was here, but he has to work."

Casey says, "Yeah, I know. He already told me."

Their voices trail off into nothing as I stare at this guy and girl sitting a few tables away from us. The girl isn't amazingly hot, but she's pretty good-looking and has what looks to be a nice set of tits. They're all over each other. The guy is rubbing her stomach and she's running her hands through his hair. Every now and then they kiss like they're going to fuck each other right there at the table.

I guess I watch them for a while because I'm still watching them when our food comes to the table probably ten minutes later.

As he gives me my eggs, the waiter says, "Here's your special plate of scrambled eggs with nothing else in them."

I say, "Thanks."

Casey and her mom both cringe again.

He leaves after asking if we need anything else and the following conversation begins:

Casey's mom takes a bite of her blueberry pancakes and says, "So after we eat I thought just you and I could go back to your place, Casey, so we can get started on everything."

Casey says, "Yeah, that sounds good. You won't mind just dropping us off, right?"

I say, "No."

Casey's mom says, "You wouldn't want to be involved in this anyway. It's really very boring . . . unless you're a woman." Then she laughs. So does Casey.

It's right then that I realize I never want to be Casey's chauffeur again.

I chew my eggs while I stare at the guy and girl who are definitely about to go somewhere and fuck after they finish their waffles. I try to remember a time when Casey was like that, and even though the memory doesn't come easily, there definitely was a time. I decide that all bitches eventually cool down and lose interest.

Then Casey says, "I'll just give you a call tomorrow morning and maybe we can all go out and eat breakfast again or something."

Her mom says, "Well, maybe we should just play it by ear."

Casey says, "Yeah, I guess you're right."

It's right at that moment that I realize I never want to be dismissed or taken for granted by Casey or her mother again. I never want to play the role they expect of me. For a split second I feel bad for the guy who I'm sure is going to be in this situation a few years from now, but at that moment it becomes crystal clear to me that when I walk out of the Griddle, I will not be engaged to this woman's daughter.

In the following minute that passes, nobody says anything, but the blood pounding in my head and my teeth grinding down on pieces of scrambled eggs and Casey licking the jelly off her lips and the fake smile that's been on her mom's face since we walked in and the general rage that's built up in me over the course of our relationship all boils down to the following seven words:

I say, "I don't think we should get married." As the words come, I feel no immediate liberation. I feel no significant change. But something, some dark, twisted knot in the pit of my stomach that I never really even knew existed, seems to loosen up a bit—just a little bit.

Her mom says, "Excuse me?"

Casey's mouth is just hanging open, half full of chewed toast. I don't really want to say anything else so I wait for her mom to say, "Did you just say you don't want to get married?"

I say, "Yeah."

Casey's mom drops her fork on her plate, wipes the corners of her mouth with the napkin that's been in her lap since she sat down, and says, "I have never been so insulted in all of my life."

Casey still hasn't said anything.

Her mom says, "You let Casey's father and me come all the way out here, find an apartment for you to live in . . . I just . . . I can't believe it. Do you realize you've wasted over a year of Casey's life? That's a year and a half that she could have been looking for someone who actually wanted to marry her."

I try to imagine who that poor guy would have been. I picture a fatter version of myself with glasses.

Casey's on the verge of tears. She finally says, "Do you still want to be boyfriend and girlfriend?"

I feel like I'm in the seventh grade telling Amber Pearson that if she won't let me touch her pussy then I don't think we should "go" together anymore because Amanda Long said she'd let me touch hers.

I say, "No, I don't think so."

"So you want to break up?"

"Yeah, I think so."

"And not see each other anymore . . . ever?"

"Yeah."

And Casey's out of commission. She just breaks down sobbing and choking and saying, "Why?"

Casey's mom moves her chair around the table and puts an arm around her daughter. She looks at me and says, "Look what you've done." Then to Casey she says, "Everything's going to be fine, honey. You'll find a husband. This doesn't mean anything."

Casey just keeps saying, "Why?"

Casey's mom stands up, forcing Casey to stand up with her, and says, "We'll be out by the car," and walks out, leaving me with the tab. As I pay it I realize a couple of things:

1. I do actually feel kind of bad about the whole thing but I am glad that I ruined Casey's mom's favorite breakfast place in L.A. by dumping her daughter in it.

And

2. I still have to give Casey and her mom a ride back to Casey's place.

chapter twenty-four

The Drive to Casey's House

Casey's house is probably about forty-five minutes from the Griddle, thirty with no traffic. There's traffic.

Casey and her mom sit in the backseat while I drive. Casey rocks back and forth sobbing and saying, "Why?" as her mom hugs her and keeps repeating, "It's going to be fine. We'll just get to your apartment and forget all about him."

As we come to a dead stop on the 405 in minute four of our drive, I wonder why her mom didn't just tell me to go fuck myself and get a cab for her and Casey to take back to Casey's apartment. As we lurch forward again I ask her.

"Are you sure you guys don't just want to get a cab? I can drop you off at a hotel or something."

Casey's mom says, "You just broke my little girl's heart and probably ruined any chance she has at getting married for at least the next year. The least you can do is drive us back to her apartment."

I say, "Okay."

Surprisingly, the drive back to Casey's apartment isn't that uncomfortable for me. Having cut Casey loose gives me a feeling of detachment from anything she must be going through and that's comforting.

Every now and then Casey says something like, "Isn't there any way we can like just talk this through?" or "I just don't understand. Can't you give me some chance to like change?" to which I say, "No, I don't think so." Then she goes back to crying so much she can't talk or properly breathe.

Her mom throws out things like, "I can understand realizing that you don't want to be with somebody after a few months, but waiting a year and a half to end something—after you've proposed, no less . . . that's just plain rude. And after all her father and I have done for you. Well, I can tell you this much, you won't be missed at any of the Childress family functions," and, "Do you honestly think you're going to find another family as giving as ours? Because you're not. The Childresses were the best thing that ever happened to you and you're going to realize it one day, but it'll be too late because Casey will be gone. She'll be married to someone else who deserves to be part of our family."

For a second I imagine Casey fucking some other guy. It doesn't bother me at all. I imagine her sucking some other guy's cock, which gets the same reaction. The thought of her getting gangbanged by the Lakers doesn't make me mad or queasy or sad or anything at all. I go back to just imagining one guy fucking her. I start to feel sorry for the guy.

Casey snaps me out of the image by saying something new: "Is there someone else?"

And even though technically there isn't, the question makes me think immediately of Alyna and what she's doing and if the fact that I'm single would change how she felt about me at all. I say, "No."

"Then why do you want to do this? I just don't understand."

I kind of feel like I do owe her an explanation, but I know telling her the truth—that I can't stand to be around her and I hate her mother and I wish she would fuck me more—will ultimately end up with her promising to change and forcing me to give her a chance to work out our problems. I also think about explaining that I never really wanted to get engaged. Maybe telling Casey's mom that the night we got "engaged" was actually a misunderstanding, that I never actually proposed. I think about seeing the look on her face when I tell her that I just went to Casey's apartment that night because she promised to fuck me, but then never did—kind of like how I supposedly agreed to marry Casey and never will. But I decide it's not worth the effort of a conversation, so instead I just say, "I just need to be by myself."

"Then we don't have to get married. We can just date and I'll give you your space."

Her mom says, "Don't cater to him. If he doesn't want you for who you are, then you don't want him." I want to smash my car into a pole just to see Casey's mom fly through the windshield.

Casey says, "Yes, I do, Mom. I love him."

I say, "I don't want to date."

Casey says, "Then we can just be friends and like start dating when you feel comfortable with the idea of it again."

Her mom says, "You're giving him too much. If you want him back, you make him come back on your terms."

I change my mind about smashing my car into a pole. Instead, I realize I'd rather get into some kind of accident that would result in Casey's mom being trapped and me having to save her, so for the rest of her life she'd know the man who ruined her daughter's life also saved hers.

I say, "Terms? I don't want that either."

Casey says, "Then whatever you want, just like let me have a chance to give it to you."

Casey's mom says, "He doesn't deserve you, Casey. Just let it go. He's not worth it."

And I'm so sick of Casey begging, and her mom being a cunt, and my imaginary car crash scenarios that I decide to just come out and say it. "Okay, you want to know what I want?"

She says, "Yes," truly believing that whatever it is I'm about to say is going to show her the way to keep me forever.

I say, "Okay, I want to fuck twice a day minimum or at least have my dick sucked. I want you to swallow. I want to butt-fuck you every once in a while and I want you to like it. . . ."

By this point I'm sure her mom is having an aneurysm, but I can't stop. I feel like every word I say should have been said a million times before over the course of our relationship. I feel like every word I say should come as no shock to Casey, but I know they do. I feel like every word I say makes up for every load I should have shot in our relationship.

For those reasons I keep saying, ". . . I never want you to tell me a stupid fucking story about shit I couldn't care less about again. I want you to get rid of your cats. I want you to lose about fifteen pounds off your ass. I want you to never want to get married or have kids. I want you to like video games. I want you to think retards are funny. I want you to not care if I say 'fuck' in front of your mom. I want you to wish Marie Osmond was dead."

The Marie Osmond line is too much for Casey's mom. She says, "Why would you ever want Marie Osmond dead? She's one of the most courageous women of our time."

I remember a line from some shitty movie Casey made me watch a month or two ago because it was one of her favorites. I decide to use the line on her. "I guess I just want you to be something you're not."

I don't know if she remembers that the line is from the movie or not, but she goes back to crying. Her mom goes back to hugging her and telling her that everything's going to be okay, and I turn up the volume on my stereo and listen to Dr. Dre's "Can't Make a Ho a Housewife," which I'm pretty sure makes me smile.

some chapter

Veggie Love

I start my hunt for Internet pornography by going to Pengus-Picks. Pengus-Picks always has at least a few clips that interest me on the site itself as well as several links to other portals. After downloading a few clips from the main site, I click a link to one of the portals. Then I click on a link that reads "U GOTTA C THIS."

I'm taken to a page that has three free movie clips: cucunt.mpg, squashfuck.avi, and cantaloupe.mpg. The idea of bitches ramming vegetables in their cunts doesn't necessarily turn me on, but the novelty of it is interesting enough for me to download all three clips.

Cucunt.mpg is forty seconds long and depicts a woman sliding a sizable cucumber in and out of her cunt three times before inserting it in her anus and then licking it.

Squashfuck.avi is fourteen seconds long and depicts a man inserting a small squash into the cunt of the same woman from cucunt.mpg.

Cantaloupe.mpg is thirty-two seconds long and depicts a different woman forcing a small but entire cantaloupe into her cunt and wincing in pain.

Despite the fact that I don't actually find the idea of women using vegetables as dildos arousing, there is something about the looks on their faces as they're doing it and the idea of using something that you normally eat as a misshapen dildo that gives me a hard-on.

I loop the clips in my Windows Media Player and jerk off. I get through the second playing of the third clip, cantaloupe.mpg, before I shoot a load that goes all over my hand.

As I get up to get some toilet paper from the bathroom, the phone rings. I answer it with my clean hand. It's my mom. She wants to know if I got the sweater she mailed to me and she wants to know if it fits.

The sweater is sitting next to my dresser in the box it was mailed in, still unopened. I say, "Yeah, I got it. It fits fine."

My mom says, "You'll wear it then?"

"Yeah."

"Good, because sometimes I buy you things even though I know you probably won't wear them." The semen is dripping down my hand.

"Mom, I need to go."

"Why? What're you doing?"

"Nothing, I just need to get going."

"All right. Well, I just wanted to make sure that sweater will work and I miss you and I love you."

"You, too."

"I also wanted to see when you were thinking about coming to visit next."

"I don't know. I'd have to check my work schedule." The semen is about to drip off my hand onto the floor.

"Well, check it when you can and let us know."

"Okay."

"Well . . . I guess good-bye then. I love you."

"I love you, too."

"Bye."

"Bye."

The semen drips off my hand onto the floor. I hang up the phone, wipe my hand with some toilet paper, and get the spot that dripped on the carpet. Then I try on the sweater. It fits.

chapter twenty-five

The Day After

I wake up, turn on the TV, and jerk off to an episode of *Real World vs. Road Rules* in which the contestants are involved in a challenge that requires the girls to wear bikinis. I get dressed and go to the gym. On my way there, I imagine fucking every girl I pass. I imagine some of them sucking my cock before I fuck them. When I finish working out there are twenty-six messages on my cell phone. I dial my voice mail and listen to the following:

"Just give me a chance. We don't have to like get married if you don't want to, not right now at least." End of message. "Call me when you get this, I have to talk to you. I just like don't understand why you're doing this." End of message. "Don't ignore me. I know you're there and I have to talk to you. Call me as soon as you get this." End of message. "My mother and I are going to get something to eat, so if you call in the next thirty minutes and we're not here, call back." End of message. "I just wanted to say that I can change. If there's something you think I'm not giving you, I can give it to you. If you still care about me at all, just call me back." End of message.

And it continues for the next ten minutes. I listen to every message, waiting to hear something that will trigger any feeling in me at all. She's crying on some of the messages, mean on others, pleading on others, but in none of them does she say anything that elicits any emotional response from me.

I delete the messages and play World of Warcraft for the next four hours. My phone rings every ten minutes for the duration of my game and each time I let it go to voice mail.

I take a ten-minute shit during which my phone rings three more times and then I listen to the new messages. Two are from Casey. The other one is from my mom. She says she forgot to ask me when Casey and I are coming to visit them again. She also wants to know if it's okay to sell all of my old He-Man toys at her next garage sale. She asks me this question once a year and my answer is always no. I delete the messages and put on a DVD called *Cum Drenched Butt Sluts*. I select scene number eight, an anal fucking and blow job scene that's been my favorite for some time.

Despite the number of times I've seen this exact scene, the look on the woman's face when the guy takes his cock out of her ass and puts it in her mouth still entertains me. She clearly doesn't like the way it tastes and she clearly doesn't like the way he rams it into the back of her throat, nor does she like the way he shoots a load of semen in her eyes and hair. I find this scene entertaining in a way that has never aroused me or made me want to jerk off. The scene that follows features two women fucking one guy. This scene does make me want to jerk off. As I start to, the phone rings again. I turn up the volume on my TV and decide to finally talk to Casey as I jerk off to this scene, hoping she'll hear the fucking in the background and wondering if I'll be able to maintain any kind of coherent conversation as I cum.

I answer the phone. It's not Casey. It's Alyna. I stop jerking off and turn down the volume as fast as I can, but I'm pretty sure she heard the guy say, "I'm gonna wreck that hole."

She makes no mention of it as she says, "Hi."

"Hi."

"Listen, I know this is probably really weird to you, but would you want to go get something to eat sometime?"

It is weird to me, she's right. But it's not weird enough to make me forget about how much I want to fuck her. "Yeah, but what about your boyfriend?"

"He's not my boyfriend anymore. What about your fiancée?"

"She's not my fiancée anymore. She never really was."

"I just, I don't know, I thought there was something between us that night, you know?"

"Yeah."

"I mean, I didn't dump my boyfriend over it or anything. We were headed in that direction anyway, but I just—I kind of felt something that night and I thought I'd give it another try, a real try, if you wanted to. And now you're single, too?"

"Yeah."

"Well, then it just kind of seems like we should at least give it a real try, right?"

"Yeah."

My call waiting goes off as Alyna and I make plans for our second date. I ignore it. After the plans have been made I turn my phone off, restart the scene on the *Cum Drenched Butt Sluts* DVD after the butt-fucking and throat fuck, restart jerking off and finish to a part that features the two bitches in the scene doing the sixty-nine while the guy fucks the top bitch doggie style and occasionally gets his balls licked by the bitch on the bottom.

I wonder if I could get Casey to do the sixty-nine with another bitch while I fucked them by telling her it's the only way I'd take her back. I wonder if she knows any girls who would do the sixty-nine with her. I somehow think Alyna might be more likely to.

some chapter

Rubbernecking

I'm driving through Westwood looking for parking when I see a bitch walking down the street. I can't tell if she's hot or not. I have to know if she's got decent tits or a redeemable ass. I have to know. So I take a good three-second stare at her. She's probably about forty-five, droopy tits, flabby ass, and haggish in the face.

I look back to the road just in time to see my front bumper make contact with the back bumper of the car in front of me that's sitting at a red light. We both pull over next to the Fatburger and get out to check the damage to our cars and exchange information.

The guy who was driving the other car says, "I was stopped at a red light. What the hell were you doing?"

"I was looking at a woman walking down the street."

"What?"

"Sorry."

"Sorry? You had your head so far up some woman's ass you didn't see my car stopped right in front of you, and all you can say is sorry?"

"Your car looks okay."

He looks it over, sees I'm right, and says, "It might look like superficial scratches, but who knows what damage we can't see."

As the guy keeps talking about the cost of what possible damages I might have done to his car, I see the woman who caused this whole thing waiting for her crosswalk sign to turn green. She's worse than I originally thought. She is hideously ugly and her body is absolutely repulsive. I smashed into a car for her.

The guy's still talking about something as I try to think about all the times I've been in near wrecks because I was trying to see if some bitch walking down the street was hot. There are a lot, and in most instances the bitch is not worth the possibility of a wreck.

The guy says, "Here." He's waving something in my face. It's his insurance information. I take his, give him mine, and wish that old hag would have at least been a hot college bitch wearing tight pants.

chapter twenty-six

Letter from Casey's Mom

It's been a few days since I dumped Casey and she's finally stopped calling. When I come home from the gym, there's an envelope with my name on it taped to the front door of my apartment. I try to remember what Casey's handwriting looks like but can't.

When I open the envelope I find out that it's not from Casey, it's from her mom, and this is what it says:

Dear Breaker of My Daughter's Heart,

I know you might find it strange that I'm writing you a letter instead of Casey, but you should know she's finally come to her senses and decided to never speak to you again after what you did. I told her she should write you a letter just so she could get out everything she needs to get out, but she refused. Well, I don't quite have the same restraint.

I can't believe you dated my daughter for so long and even went so far as to propose to her only to end things the way you did. You are the most miserable and ungrateful person I think I may have ever had the displeasure of meeting and I for one have absolutely no regrets that my daughter didn't wind up marrying the likes of you. My only regret is that she wasted so much of her own time and so much of her family's time on you.

I consider myself lucky because Casey's sister has found a man who loves her for who she is and has been able to give me a grandchild. But I also consider myself very unlucky in that I'm not positive Casey will ever be able to give me the joy of a grandchild because I'm sure it will be a long time before she's ready to try men again and you're to blame. I hope that stays with you.

Just for the record, when Casey told us she was engaged to you, I was not immediately happy, and even after trying to convince myself that it was a good thing, I was never fully satisfied with my daughter bringing someone like you into our family and neither was Casey's father.

I wish that I could somehow warn every woman on the planet what a cruel and unfeeling person you are so in the future other girls won't suffer the same misery my daughter has, but after witnessing your behavior this weekend in the Griddle I have no doubt that you will remain alone for the rest of your life, and that thought comforts me a great deal.

In closing I'd just like to let you know that when you come to your senses in a month or so and realize that you threw away the best thing that ever happened to you by ending your relationship with my daughter and with the Childress family, it will be too late. Casey will never accept your apology and neither will I. You have made the biggest mistake of your life.

Sincerely,
Anne Childress

I fold the letter back up and put it back in its envelope. I know I will probably never read the letter again, but something makes me want to keep it, so I put it in the latest issue of Playboy, which is sitting on my coffee table.

As I take a shower I wonder if I should write Casey's mom a response letter. I decide against it based on the lack of interest I have in ever communicating with her again. I wonder if I should write a letter to Casey. I decide against this based on the possibility that Casey might misinterpret something I write as a chance to get back together and start calling me every five minutes again.

In the shower I reach for the soap and notice Casey's sponge thing. I remember a specific time we fucked in my shower and she washed my cock with that sponge thing after we finished. I wash my cock with her sponge thing and get an immediate hard-on, but refuse to jerk off on principle.

chapter twenty-seven

Psychosis

It's 2:32 A.M. and I'm walking toward the front door of my apartment building after a long and unsuccessful night of playing wingman for Todd while he tried to pick up bitches at the Westwood Brewing Company. I see something that almost makes me fake an aneurysm so I don't have to deal with it. Casey's sitting outside the front doors by the call box. She's already seen me and there's nothing I can do. Even though I know the following conversation is unavoidable, I try to pretend I don't see her sitting in front of the door I have to walk through as I reach for my keys in preparation to enter.

She says, "I've been sitting out here like all night. Even though my mom told me not to, I had to come over here. Where have you been?"

"Out with Todd."

"I can't do this. I don't know how to do this."

"Do what?"

"Not be us."

She starts crying like a little kid. I don't say anything. I just stand there watching her sob and wondering how I'm ever going to get her off my porch without actually calling the police and having her forcibly removed.

She says, "Why? Why do you want to do this to me?"

I still don't say anything. It's becoming even more apparent to me that this situation could very quickly unfold into the worst moment of my life.

"I just don't understand it."

I still don't say anything.

"Say something."

I say, "Uh, it's pretty late and I'm tired. Maybe we could talk about this later."

"I came all the way over here and sat on your porch for five hours. I'm not leaving until you talk to me."

I don't say anything. I put my key in the door, open it, and walk in. Casey just sits there. I go to my apartment and look out the window at Casey, still sitting there. I watch her for five minutes. She doesn't move except to cry every now and then. Then she stands up and starts screaming.

She says, "You fucking bastard! I hate you and I'm not leaving here until you talk to me! Just come out and talk to me!"

I go into my bathroom and take a long-overdue shit as Casey keeps screaming on the front porch. I'm sure some of my neighbors can hear her screaming but she never uses my name, so I don't care. She just keeps screaming things like, "You're a fucking son of a bitch," and "I'm sorry I ever let you have sex with me," followed by, "I just want to talk," and "Please give me a chance to work it out."

As I wipe my ass she's still screaming. When I get out of the shower she's still screaming. When I get in bed, she's still screaming. When I jerk off thinking about the possibilities of fucking Alyna on our next date, she's still screaming.

I wonder if she'll be asleep on my front porch when I leave for work tomorrow morning or if someone will call the cops before then or if she'll just get tired and go home.

some chapter

UCLA Party

Todd and another friend of mine whose last name is Marquis are over at my house. We've been drinking beer for the last three hours and playing Madden when Marquis makes the following suggestion: "Dude, we should go to a fucking college party around here."

Todd says, "Do you think we can even pass as college-age anymore?"

Marquis says, "Fuck it. Who gives a shit if we can? What're they gonna do, fucking kick us out?"

I say, "They might."

Marquis says, "So we fuckin' leave then. But if they don't kick us out—free fuckin' booze and free fuckin' eighteen-year-old pussy."

Todd says, "Fuck it, I'm in, dude."

I agree. We all knock back one for the road and walk out the door in search of a party in the area. As we walk Todd says, "So once we get to a party, what's our story?"

Marquis says, "We're fuckin' baseball players from USC. One of our friends who transferred to UCLA last semester invited us over here."

I say, "What do we tell 'em when they ask who the friend is?"

Marquis says, "Fuckin' Jim."

Todd says, "Jim?"

Marquis says, "Fuckin' Jim. There's always a fuckin' Jim at a party, dude."

Marquis' logic is apparently sound enough for Todd and me because we don't ask any more questions before we find ourselves walking up the steps to an apartment from which loud music and drunk college bitches pour out onto the balcony.

We walk in seemingly undetected and make our way to the kitchen where a keg is being pumped by a gigantic thick-necked guy who is either fat or muscular—I'm not sure which. Thick-neck says, "Where's your cup, bra?"

Marquis says, "Some bitch knocked it outta my hand on the fuckin' balcony."

Thick-neck gives him a new cup. "Bros before hos. Here you go, bro." Marquis gets a cup full of beer from Thick-neck, then says, "My buddies here lost their shit, too." Thick-neck supplies us with beer and continues to pump the keg as we walk off into the pitch-black living room.

I sit down on a couch next to a hot bitch and start to notice that Todd, Marquis, and myself are the shortest guys at the party by at least a foot and underweigh all the guys at the party by at least a hundred pounds. The hot bitch says, "Hey, who are you?"

I say, "A friend of Jimmy's."

"Oh."

I can't believe it fucking worked.

The hot bitch says, "Are you on the football team?"

"No, I play baseball for USC."

"Oh, cool. Freshman?"

"Sophomore, you?"

"I'm a sophomore too—on the soccer team. It's kind of noisy in here, do you want to go out on the balcony?"

"Sure."

She takes my hand and we go out on the balcony, where there are three other guys and three other girls. The guys all seem to be bigger than the ones inside. They shoot me a look when they see me. The hot bitch notices and says, "He plays baseball for USC." The guys' scowls turn to head nods and a few guys say things like, "Cool," and "Baseball, a'ight," before turning back to their respective college sluts and getting back to trying to fuck them.

The hot bitch says, "So how do you like L.A.?"

"Okay, you?"

"I'm originally from Phoenix, but I like it here okay. Do you have a girlfriend at USC?"

"No. You have a boyfriend?"

"No. I did, but now I don't."

"Oh."

"Yeah, it's cool now though. He was a complete asshole. You probably saw him in there pumping the keg."

I immediately picture Thick-neck tossing me off the balcony or caving in my fucking skull with the keg.

"Yeah, I think I saw him."

"Well, we're through, even if he doesn't think so."

I look back inside and see that Marquis and Todd are talking to a few hot bitches of their own and know there's no way they'll leave this party. I'm fucked. I say, "I feel kind of sick, I think I should go to the bathroom."

She takes my hand and says, "The line's probably horrible. You can use the one in my bedroom."

She leads me through the living room crowd, thankfully out of Thick-neck's line of sight, and into her bedroom, closing and locking the door behind her. She lies down on her bed and points to the adjoining bathroom. She says, "Bathroom's in there."

I go in, look in the mirror, can't draw a bead on my face—still too drunk. Fuck it. I walk back into her bedroom and say, "I really think I should go."

She shakes her head and pats the bed beside her. "No, stay here for a few more minutes. You'll feel better. I promise."

Two things fight for dominance in my head: this hot bitch's tight eighteen-year-old ass and Thick-neck's fists. The ass wins by a landslide. I sit down. She starts kissing me and shoots a hand down my pants. Forty-five seconds later, she's sucking my cock. I wonder if she wants to fuck and I wonder if she has any rubbers. I'm about to ask her when somebody knocks at the door. "Cammie, come dance with me." It's fucking Thick-neck.

She rolls her eyes, takes my cock out of her mouth, and says, "Richard, I don't want to dance with you."

"Come on, babe. It's your favorite song." I try to listen to the song through the door to gain some insight into what kind of an eighteen-year-old college slut Cammie might be, but it's too garbled.

I look around for a window, but strangely Cammie doesn't have one. I am positive I'm going to die at the hands of Richard the thick-necked keg pumper.

He says, "Cammie, come on, just one dance."

Cammie does a few more head bobs on my cock, then says, "Okay, I'm feeling kind of sick, just give me fifteen minutes, then I'll give you one dance."

He says, "All right, babe. I'll be at the keg if you feel better sooner."

She says, "I fucking hate that asshole," then gets right back to work on my cock. It's a fairly well-executed blow job. I've had better, but not many. As Cammie starts to play with my balls I kind of wish I was getting a blow job from the twenty-four-year-old version of Cammie so she'd have a little more experience, but then my thoughts come back to the fact that I'm getting my dick sucked by an eighteen-year-old hot college bitch and I'm about to blow my load.

I say, "Do you have any condoms?"

She stops sucking my cock and says, "I want you to finish in my mouth."

I have no problem with this. I say, "Okay."

As she sucks my cock, I assume that she's just into swallowing. But after I shoot my load in her mouth and then sneak back out into the party and watch her give Richard his promised dance as well as a minute-long tongue-kiss, I realize she was just using me.

chapter twenty-eight

Second Date

I ring Alyna's doorbell for a second time, meet her hippie roommate for a second time, make small talk for a second time, and wait for Alyna to come out of what I assume is her bedroom for a second time.

She walks in front of me out of her apartment complex and I see that her ass is as good as I remember. I decide that if tonight leads to any point at which there might be even a remote possibility I can fuck her or get her to suck my cock, I'll try my best to make sure it happens.

We get in my car and I reach to put the keys in the ignition. She grabs my hand, stops me, and says, "Does this feel kind of weird to you?"

"No."

"Really?"

"I don't know, maybe a little."

"It feels really weird to me."

Fuck. It's over before it even started.

I say, "You want to call it off?"

"No. No. It's not necessarily weird in a bad way."

She squeezes my hand and I feel her fingers, kind of hard and wiry. I wish those fingers were squeezing my dick.

She says, “Let’s go.”

I start up the car and we head off. The ride is pretty uneventful. We never really address either of our breakups or how we felt about our first date. She tells me about last night’s episode of Conan O’Brien, which I missed, and I tell her about the new 50 Cent video. At one point she laughs at something I say and puts her hand on my shoulder as she’s laughing, which forces her to turn her tits at me. That’s when I notice the button-up shirt she’s wearing gives me a slight glimpse of one of her tits. I take it in. It’s nice. I want to be sucking it.

We get to the Smoke House in Burbank, which I remember Casey taking me to a few times. It’s an interesting place if nothing else and if the date itself goes sour, the senior citizen lounge act will be entertaining.

We get a table kind of by the stage and order a few drinks to start the following conversation:

She says, “So why’d you and your girlfriend break up?”

“She thought we were getting married and I didn’t.”

“I guess that’s a pretty big thing to disagree about.”

“Yeah, I guess so. Why’d you and your boyfriend break up?”

“He was a complete dick and I was tired of dating a complete dick.”

I wonder what it was about him that made him a complete dick. I don’t ask her. I’m sure I’m fully capable of duplicating whatever it was. I just say, “Fair enough.”

She says, “Do you think it’s too soon to be dating other people?”

“No.”

“My boyfriend and I were dating for almost a year and a half, and I know you’re supposed to have some time by yourself before you jump back into dating and all that, but I don’t really feel like I need any time. I’m over him. I was over him while we were dating. What do you think?”

"I'm pretty much the same way."

We get our drinks. She raises her glass and says, "Let's do a toast."

"To what?"

"To . . ." She thinks. ". . . seeing what happens."

"Sounds good."

We clink glasses and drink.

We talk about a lot of things through the course of our dinner and have at least three more drinks each. I find out she's a senior at UCLA. She has two brothers—one is older and lives in New York and does something on Wall Street and the other is one year younger and plays baseball at Arizona State. Her mom and dad were high school sweethearts who still live in the town they were born in. She's twenty-one but has never gotten a driver's license. She's only been in two serious relationships. She won't give the exact number of people she's slept with, but it's under ten. She has freckles on her shoulders. When she was seven years old she found nine hundred dollars in a garbage bag behind the dumpster in her alley. When she was ten her brother threw the metal lid of a coffee can at her like a Frisbee and it cut the two middle fingers on her left hand to the bone. As a result she has no feeling in the tips of those fingers.

I tell her similar information about myself and the date seems to be going well. When she gets up to go to the bathroom, I watch her ass and think about it naked spread over my face as we do the sixty-nine.

When she comes back, she puts a hand on my shoulder as she walks around the table, which I take as a good sign.

She says, "So you ready to hit the road?"

"Sure." I pay the bill and we leave.

In the car she says, "So do you want to check out my apartment? My roommate's supposed to be spending the night at some camp-out thing."

"Yeah."

Although this kind of offer would normally mean a girl is ready to be fucked, I can't be sure because of the strange circumstances surrounding the date and her behavior on our first date. Nonetheless, it's well worth my time to see what happens.

Once we get inside her apartment she gives me the grand tour, ending at her bedroom, which is decorated in a pretty normal college girl kind of way. There are more pillows than necessary on her bed, a poster of Einstein on her wall, and a little bookshelf with college philosophy books and classic literature on it. In the corner she has a thirteen-inch TV.

She sits on her bed and slips her shoes off. I notice a picture stuck in her mirror of her and her ex-boyfriend. I wonder if she forgot to take it down or if she left it up on purpose. I don't ask.

She says, "Do you want to watch some TV?"

"Okay."

She turns on her TV and I sit down next to her on her bed, closer than I need to. She doesn't move away. She says, "You know, I'm sorry about our first date."

I don't know why I say it, but it seems right to say, "Me too."

She leans in and kisses me. It's a good kiss, one that makes me ready to fuck her immediately. I reach up and put my hand behind her head, and she does the same to me. We kiss for a few seconds before she lies down, taking me with her.

Then she stops and says, "Wait."

Fuck.

Then she sits up, unbuttons her shirt, and takes off her bra.

Fuck yes.

Her tits are un-fucking-believable, rock hard, perfectly round B cups. She takes my hands and puts them on her tits, then kind of moans. She drops back down on top of me and we start going at it. She half rips my shirt off and unzips my pants before I know what the fuck is going on. She shoves her hand down my pants and starts jerking me off. It's been a long time since I've been with a girl who's this enthusiastic about dick. For a split second I'm sure I'm going to blow a load in my pants, but I hold it back.

As she's tugging at my cock, I reach down and unzip her pants, which she helps me take off. She lets go of my dick for a second and pulls off her underwear before yanking off my pants and boxers so we're both completely naked in her bed. Despite the number of times I've jerked off to this exact fantasy, I never imagined it could be this good.

My cock is harder than I can remember it being in a long time when she starts jerking at it again.

She says, "This is what I wanted to do the first time we went out."

"Me too."

"I'm glad we didn't, though."

"Me too." I say it without really knowing what the fuck I'm saying or what that could even mean. All I can focus on is her hand on my cock.

She says, "Do you like it soft," and she kind of teases my dick with her fingers, "or hard," then she squeezes my cock and yanks on it kind of hard.

The fact that she's so aggressive and vocal about this entire event is again about to make me blow my load, so I take the opportunity to shift my focus to her.

I slide a few fingers into her pussy, which is already pretty wet, and say, "How do you like it?"

She kind of grinds on my hand at her own pace and I give as much resistance as I think she might like.

She says, "Just like that," with her hand still on my cock, but not as intent on jerking me off.

I finger her for a while listening to her moan and feeling her hand on my cock until I feel her pull away. I've gotten enough head to know that as she starts kissing me on the neck and then on the chest that her mouth's headed for my dick.

A few seconds later I'm not disappointed as she has one hand on my balls and her mouth on my cock. It's a pretty good blow job. Not quite the best I've ever had, but definitely good. I stop wondering if this is going to be a precursor to fucking when I realize I'm about to cum. I reach down and squeeze her shoulder to give her fair warning, but she keeps sucking and right as I cum she squeezes my nuts a little, which is a new experience for me and not unenjoyable, then swallows the entire load I shoot in her mouth with a little giggle. This is more than pleasantly surprising. It confirms my hopes that Alyna is a girl who not only genuinely enjoys sucking cock, but also fully enjoys all aspects of the act. She keeps sucking my cock for a minute or so after I've shot my load, which is also a new experience for me that I find much more enjoyable than the nut squeeze.

When she finishes she crawls back up and lies next to me on her back, rubbing my chest and kissing me on the neck in a way that lets me know she's ready for her turn.

I spread her legs and bury my face in her cunt, which is easily the best-looking pussy I've ever seen. It's well trimmed and neat with smallish lips and a decent taste. I flick my tongue at her clit for a few seconds before really going to work and putting a few fingers in her as I eat her out. After twenty or thirty seconds of this, she's kind of writhing around and moaning with her hands on my head pulling my face deeper into her pussy. She accidentally pulls a little too hard once and hits my nose against her pubic bone, which hurts a little, but not enough to stop me from doing my work.

Once she gets completely worked up and she's about to cum, she pushes me away, rolls over on her stomach, gets up on all fours with her ass in the air and her legs spread so her pussy's kind of open and sticking out.

She says, "I want to cum like this."

I've only ever seen a guy eat a girl out from behind in a porno movie, but I have nothing against it as I spread Alyna's ass from behind, which I'm dumbfounded by when I look at how perfect it is again. I get off the bed slightly so my face is at her ass level and pull her back so she's still on all fours at the edge of the bed as I lick her cunt from the back.

She keeps backing into my face as I'm eating her out, which causes my nose to actually touch her asshole. I'm surprised to find that it smells good, kind of like pears or some kind of berry. I wonder if she uses scented toilet paper or actually sprays some kind of body spray in her asshole on a regular basis, or maybe she just thought that at some point tonight she'd wind up with my nose in her ass so she used the spray, based on an educated guess.

Her nice-smelling asshole makes me less apprehensive about really cutting loose, and a few times I notice my tongue getting a stray lick in on the asshole itself, which she seems to genuinely enjoy. This makes me think that at some point I could possibly fuck her in the ass.

My neck starts to hurt from the weird angle my head's suspended at but her perfect ass in my face and her escalating moaning makes me want to finish her off like this. So I continue for a few more minutes, ignoring the burning pain.

Right after one of her loudest moans she says, "Spank me."

Holy shit. I have spanked girls I've fucked in the past and some have even liked it. But none have demanded it of me. I hit one of her ass cheeks.

She says, "Harder."

I hit her harder.

She says, "Again."

I get in about seven or eight solid slaps before she cums like a ton of bricks, shudders a little, and then collapses in a heap on her bed. She rolls over on her back and I lie down next to her.

She says, "That was great."

"Yeah, it was."

I'm kind of curious as to why we didn't fuck, but more than curious I'm refreshed by the immensely satisfying and enthusiastic blow job she delivered and her clearly expressed and unique preference for being eaten out.

Just before we both fall asleep I wonder if Alyna will fall in love with me.

chapter twenty-nine

Post-Lunch with Carlos

After eating the same lunch we eat every Saturday at the CPK in the Beverly Center, Carlos and I are across the street at the music store in the Beverly Connection in the DVD section shopping for his mom's birthday present.

Carlos holds up the Vin Diesel *Pacifier* DVD and says, "You think my mom would like this? I would love to suck his cock."

"I'm sure he'd love that."

"You never know. Anyway that's neither here nor there. I still can't believe you and Casey are kaput. I mean, despite all the shit you always complained about, I thought you guys would wind up married—maybe divorced down the line, but married at some point. That is funny though about her mom writing you that letter. Do you still have it?"

"Yeah."

"I want to read it. I love shit like that." He picks up a *Spider-Man* DVD and says, "I think I remember my mom telling me that she and my dad saw this movie like three or four times." He flips the DVD over and reads the back as he says, "Tobey Maguire . . . I'd suck his dick so fucking good."

"Is he gay?"

"You don't have to be gay to have your dick sucked." He looks through some more DVDs and then says, "And you still haven't talked to her since she showed up at your house stalker-style?"

"No."

"Jesus fucking Christ, that's pretty cold. But maybe it's for the best. You don't want her getting the idea that you want her back in your life if you don't. I fucked this one little Chinese hardbody for about a week and a half before I got sick and tired of getting poked by his two-inch pushpin and dumped him on Valentine's Day. But I kept talking to him, you know, just to be nice, and he somehow thought that meant he could drop by anytime and try to make me cum with his little nub. Jesus, that was a long two weeks. Anyway, like I was saying, it's probably better you don't talk to her."

"I agree."

He holds up an *Assassins* DVD and says, "My mom likes Stallone. Do you think either one of these guys would let me suck their cock?"

"I don't know."

"And now what's the deal with this new girl? She sucked your dick and you ate her out, and she's the same one you went on that other date with?"

"Right."

"Do you think it's a little quick to be jumping right back into another cunt?"

"I'm not jumping into anything. It was just a date."

"For me, wrapping my lips around a cock is just a date. For any girl, though, sucking some guy's dick is not just a date. Didn't you say she just got out of some long-term relationship, too?"

"Yeah."

"I don't know. I mean, don't get me wrong, I'm all for getting off as much as you possibly can in this life, but this looks like trouble to me."

"Trouble was being engaged to Casey. If Alyna's trouble, at least she's trouble with a perfect fucking ass."

He holds up *Ace Ventura* and says, "She hates Jim Carrey. Maybe I should get her this. I don't know why, but I've always had a crush on him. I think it has something to do with that scene in the second one when he crawls out of that rhino's ass naked." He puts the DVD back on the shelf and says, "I mean, did she snuggle up to you after you guys finished or did you guys fall asleep together or anything?"

"We fell asleep in her bed, but we weren't snuggled up or anything."

"Did she touch you at all?"

"Yeah. She has a small bed. It couldn't be helped."

"Then in the morning what happened?"

"I got up and left."

"Jesus, did you even say, 'Thanks for the blow job?'"

"I kissed her and we both said we had a good time and all that, then I left."

"Well, just be careful. After getting out of something like you had with Casey, I think it's very easy to fall right back into the same trap if you don't watch out. And you didn't even give me any time to convince you that women are all evil bitches and you should give guys a try."

He laughs at his joke, then picks up a *Wizard of Oz* DVD and says, "This is it. She fucking loves this stupid movie. So many fags love it, too, but I fucking hate it. All those little midgets and that fucking song that every guy I've ever fucked knows by heart and actually starts fucking singing when we're watching it. I don't know how many times I've had to sit through this piece of shit just so I could get some cock up my ass. I almost don't want to buy it on principle alone, but . . I'm getting it. My mom will like it. You getting anything?"

"No."

At the register, the girl ringing us up is hot as fuck in that indie-rock-slightly-Emo just-out-of-high-school kind of way. Nice little tits, dyed black hair, nose ring, tattoo peeking out of her shirt and probably weighs a hundred pounds. I immediately imagine myself fucking her doggie style in some back room of the record store. A few seconds in, I start thinking about Alyna in the back room of the record store and end up continuing to think about her all the way back to my house, where I jerk off to the memory of her sucking my cock.

chapter thirty

Casey's Shit

Casey hasn't tried to call me for almost a week, which is why it kind of surprises me when I pick up the phone and hear her say with forced confidence, "When's a good time for me to come get the things I have at your apartment?"

"Uh, I don't know."

"Well, I have some stuff that I need to get back. You can't keep it."

I don't think she does have anything at my apartment, but after a year and a half of dating it makes sense that she would, so I don't argue.

"When do you want to come get it?"

"Today if I can."

"Okay. I'll be here."

"I'll be over in an hour."

She hangs up. I think about finding whatever shit she's talking about and putting it all in a box on the curb so she can just take it and go instead of hanging around my apartment longer than necessary, but I don't really know which shit is hers and I'd probably end up giving her something of mine by mistake, which she'd take to mean something it didn't. I'm also fully aware that this is, more than likely, just a ploy for her to see me again, maybe in hopes of luring me back to her fat ass. I hope that playing along will give her some sort of closure so I never have to see her again. I decide I should play an old Xbox game. I decide to play Mech Assault 2 until she shows up, which turns out to be an hour later.

When she comes in she says, "I'm sorry about that night I showed up here. How have you been?"

"Okay."

"So have I. I started my next Groundlings class."

"Great. I didn't know which stuff you were talking about."

"I didn't think you would."

She rummages through a pile of papers and *Playboys* on my coffee table. Her mom's letter falls out onto the ground and she picks it up.

"Is this from my mom?"

"Yeah."

"What is it?"

"A letter."

"Obviously it's a letter, but like why would she write you a letter?"

I shrug my shoulders, knowing she wants to read it more than anything. She puts it back in the *Playboy*, closes the magazine, and tosses it down on the coffee table a little too nonchalantly.

"My Groundlings teacher said I have the most potential of anyone in the class."

"Great. Do you know exactly what you have over here?"

"Just some things."

She goes in the closet and pulls out an umbrella that I think my mom gave me when I moved to L.A.

She says, "Like my umbrella."

She opens a cupboard in the kitchen area, pulls out a box of tea, and says, "And my tea."

She walks back into the bedroom and comes out still holding just the tea and the umbrella. She says, "Are you doing anything right now?"

Fuck. I should have just thrown some of my shit in a box and left it on the curb.

"No."

"Do you want to go get a cup of coffee with me?"

"I don't think so."

"Just like to talk."

"I don't think so."

"Why?"

"I just don't want to."

"It's because I came over to your house and yelled at you and now you think I'm a psycho."

"No, I just don't want to."

"Well, then, let's have dinner this week."

"I don't think I can."

"Why can't you just have dinner with me and talk to me about this whole thing?"

"It's better like this."

"Like what?"

"Just over."

"No, it's not."

"Sorry."

She starts to tear up. She starts crying. She says through sobs, "Aren't you even going to hug me?"

I wish I was anywhere else. I think about Alyna. I think about telling Casey that I ate Alyna's pussy and she sucked my cock.

"I don't think so."

Her sobs become convulsive. She sits down on my couch and cries into her hands.

"Why? I just like don't understand why."

I don't say anything.

"Can you just tell me why you're doing this?"

"I already did."

"Because you want something I'm not?"

"Yeah."

"That doesn't even like make sense. I was something you wanted for a year and a half and now I'm just not? What happened?"

"I don't know."

"You have to know. If you broke up with me you have to know."

I don't say anything again. I know that anything I say will only prolong this already annoying situation.

"I mean there has to be something that changed."

I stand as still as I can and try not to breathe. For a split second I think I might be able to coax her into sucking my cock or fucking me, but it's probably not worth the effort.

She says, "It was the engagement, wasn't it?"

Please something happen. A car wreck right outside my door. A gunshot through my window. A fucking phone call for fuck's sake. As I think this my cell phone actually rings. Casey sits on the couch, still crying as I answer it. It's Alyna, who I've only talked to once in the two days since she sucked my cock.

She says, "What're you doing?"

"Nothing."

"I'm done with work. Can I come over?"

"When?"

"Now."

"I haven't taken a shower or anything."

"That's fine. Neither have I. We can take one together. I'll be over in ten minutes."

She hangs up. The slightly less than comfortable familiarity she's approaching in whatever kind of relationship we might be on the verge of having makes me a little uneasy, but the thought of soaping up her ass and tits in my shower generates a spark of excitement that alleviates it; and the crying-ex-girlfriend-sitting-on-my-couch situation seems slightly more pressing.

I say, "Okay, you have to go."

"Why?"

"Because I'm tired of arguing about this." Even as I say the words it hits me that I owe Casey nothing, but something makes me think telling her about Alyna would make the entire situation worse. I wonder if Alyna has any interaction with her ex-boyfriend and if it's similar to mine with Casey.

She says, "Well, I'm not leaving until I get an answer or until you at least promise to get coffee with me."

"Fine."

"Fine what? The answer or the coffee?"

"Coffee."

"When?"

"I'll call you."

"No, you won't."

"Yes, I will."

"You promise?"

"Yes."

"Okay, but I'm holding you to it."

She gets off my couch, wipes the tears off her face, and leaves.

I sit on the couch where she was sitting for about two or three minutes thinking about the last time Casey and I fucked. I wish I had blown a load on her stomach or put my dick in her ass or done something to signify it as the final time I would put my cock in her. Alyna rings my doorbell, shifting my thoughts back to her soapy cunt in my shower.

She walks in and says, "Hi," then kisses me, sees the tea that I now realize Casey left sitting on the coffee table along with what I am now sure is my umbrella, and says, "I would have never guessed you for a tea drinker."

The shower we take five minutes later yields a pretty good and immediate soapy hand job that leaves me no opportunity to even attempt fucking her. Instead I repay the favor by making her cum as I finger-fuck her up against my shower door. The dinner we eat afterward at Jerry's Famous Deli is filled with conversation about trivial things that ignore the nature of what seems to be a burgeoning rclationship, but nonetheless is the only conversation either of us wants to have.

some chapter

The 98 Percent Rule

Todd and I are eating lunch at a Quiznos in North Hollywood. Sitting across from us at two different tables are an unrealistically hot bitch who we decide must be a porno actress and an old lady who looks like she died two weeks ago.

Todd says, "If you had to fuck the old ugly one, but then you get to fuck the hot one, would you do it?"

"What's the rest of the scenario?"

"There is no rest. That's it."

"What about disease, and pregnancy, and subsequent chances to fuck the hot bitch?"

"No. You don't get any of that."

"See? So there's more to the situation here. You have to lay it out completely."

"Okay, here's your scenario. You're lying in bed at one A.M. and the old bitch materializes in your bed completely naked and starts sucking your cock."

"Okay."

"Now, while she sucks, she says, 'If you fuck me, not just let me suck your cock, but actually stick your dick in me, then right after you blow your load, the hot porno bitch will show up and fuck you, too.' And you get no diseases, there're no pregnancies, no one knows about it, and both bitches vaporize as soon as you blow your load."

"And I'll be magically ready to fuck immediately after I've just fucked the old bitch?"

"Yeah."

I think it over. I look at the old bitch, at her gunt, at her wrinkly, jerky lips as she eats a cup of Quiznos clam chowder. I realize that given Todd's theoretical situation I think I would fuck her even if the hot bitch wasn't a follow-up.

I say, "In your theoretical situation I'd fuck the old bitch even if there was no hot bitch."

"Dude, that is fucking vile."

"You would, too."

"What? No fucking way."

"Yeah, you would. If no one will know and there's no risk involved, what do you care if she's old. She's still got a pussy, right?"

He realizes I'm right. "Yeah, I guess I would fuck her. Would you fuck any bitch on this planet given that same situation?"

My gut reaction is to say yes, but logically that can't be true. I hedge my bet.

I say, "Maybe not all of them. In the age range of seventeen or so to dead, I'd probably fuck like ninety-eight percent."

A decent-looking mom walks in with two little kids. She's kind of fat.

Todd indicates her with a head nod and says, "Is she ninety-eight percent?"

"Yeah."

There's an old, insane-looking homeless bitch on the street corner.

Todd points to her and says, "Dude, is she ninety-eight percent?"

"Uhhh . . . yeah, sure."

"Holy shit. You'd fuck her?"

"Yeah, if she vaporizes right after I do it, what do I care?"

"If she's ninety-eight percent, then what's a two-percenter look like?"

"I don't know. I'll let you know when I see one."

We finish our sandwiches and on the entire ride back to work we don't pass a single two-percenter. I wonder if the fact that I live in Los Angeles has anything to do with it or if I should just change my range to ninety-nine percent. It's probably L.A. I decide to leave it at ninety-eight percent.

chapter thirty-one

Introducing Alyna

Over the course of the last week Alyna's sucked my cock once and given me one hand job in the shower. I've eaten her out once and fingered her once, also in my shower. These statistics are enough to make Todd want to meet her.

I pick Alyna up at nine and we go to a bar called Daddy's, where we meet Todd and two girls sitting in a booth with him who I assume did not come with him. One of the girls is short and fat with a pretty cute face and small sloppy tits that are poorly concealed in a shirt that no girl that chubby should be wearing. The other girl is surprisingly attractive for having such a fat pig as a friend. As we sit down Todd says, "What's up guys, this is Sandra and Debra."

Debra, the short fat one, says, "It's Devra, with a *v*, like vagina."

In addition to being short and fat, Devra is drunk.

I introduce Alyna to everyone around the table.

Todd says, "So, Alyna, what do you do?"

She says, "I'm a student. This is my last year, though."

Todd says, "Cool."

Sandra, the hot girl, says, "Where do you go?"

Alyna says, "UCLA."

Devra the fat pig says to me, "And are you guys like boyfriend and girlfriend or are you fair game?" Then she laughs a weird laugh that almost sounds like an eight-year-old kid and I imagine the cellulite that must be on her ass and thighs rippling as I fuck her.

Alyna looks at me. I refuse to say anything.

She says, "No, we actually both got out of relationships not too long ago and I've sucked his dick once and he's eaten me out . . . oh, and we've given each other hand jobs in his shower, but it's not that whole boyfriend-girlfriend thing yet, so I guess he's fair game."

I want to fuck Alyna right there.

Devra the fat pig looks at me with an open mouth. Judging by their similar slack-jawed expressions, Sandra and Todd also seem to be a little surprised by the bluntness of what Alyna just said. I smile and kiss Alyna on the cheek. She smiles back.

Todd says, "Uh . . . I'm going up to the bar to get some drinks. You guys want anything?"

We put in our order with Todd and he leaves us with Sandra and Devra, whose mouth is still hanging open, making her look even more like an actual pig to me.

Alyna says, "So what do you guys do?"

Devra the fat pig says, "I work at an ad agency as a project coordinator."

Sandra the hot one says, "I'm a graphic designer at the same place."

Devra says to me, "And what do you do?"

I say, "Nothing important."

That ends whatever conversation might have been about to happen. We sit in silence for another minute until Todd comes back with drinks for the whole table, which seems to erase the uneasiness everyone was feeling after Alyna told them she sucked my cock.

As we all drink and talk about nothing important, Sandra the hot girl explains that since moving to Los Angeles she's only dated jerks and can't seem to find a guy that takes her seriously. Devra the fat pig explains that all the guys she goes out with just want to have sex and then never call her again. Sandra further explains that her problem isn't in the guys calling her back. They call her all the time, it's just that they only call her to have sex. I can see Todd mentally constructing the best possible strategy to result in fucking at least one of them tonight, preferably the hot one.

He says, "I hate the dating scene. I've had my heart broken enough to know that it's rough out there, especially for a guy who just wants to meet a nice girl and doesn't want the whole fast-paced L.A. thing."

It's a strong strategy.

Alyna leans over and whispers in my ear, "Does your friend really think that's going to work?"

Sandra the hot one and Devra the fat pig say almost in unison, "I know what you mean."

I lean over and whisper in Alyna's ear, "Yes."

Alyna drinks the last of her cosmopolitan and says, "I'm getting another drink, anybody want anything?" I ask her to get me another Dewar's and then watch her perfect ass leave the table in a tight black skirt. When I turn my head back to the conversation at hand, I notice Todd was also watching Alyna's ass. He notices me noticing him and then gives me the thumbs-up. The two girls he's trying to fuck tonight are oblivious as they talk about a new lip gloss that Sandra bought at the Grove.

I look at the bar to see if Alyna's close to getting our drinks and see that some guy is talking to her. He's sloppily holding a drink and standing as close as he possibly can to her. I wonder if he's thinking about fucking her or getting his dick sucked as he tries to pick her up. My gut reaction is to go to the bar under the guise of seeing if Alyna needs help so I can tell this asshole to go fuck himself, but I don't know if that's something I have the clearance to do at this point in whatever relationship it is that we have. So I watch the following:

The guy says something to her.

She gives no reaction.

The guy says something to her again and motions his drink toward her, possibly asking if he can buy her one.

She shakes her head.

The guy says something else and Alyna looks over at me, rolls her eyes, and mouths,"I fucking hate this," as she indicates the guy with a thumb point.

It's in that one second that I have an overwhelming urge to hug her, to fall asleep with her, to wake up with her, to smell her hair, to do everything with her except fuck. Then she turns around to pick up our drinks from the bar and I get a perfect shot of her ass again, which replaces my previous impulses with the more familiar set of urges to fuck her in every way imaginable.

She comes back to the table with a fresh round of drinks. We all talk about movies, TV shows, and records we think are good and bad and other completely boring bullshit. Todd and the hot girl seem to be doing most of the talking as the fat pig tries to interject here and there but must know she has no chance of scoring any guy once her hot friend shows even the most remote amount of interest.

Neither Alyna nor I contribute much to the conversation. Instead we drink our drinks and she puts her hand in my lap. Over the course of the next thirty minutes, her hand moves from gently resting on my leg to semi–jerking me off through my pants. Todd and his two bitches are oblivious to what's going on under the table, which at one point is me fingering Alyna under her skirt and her about to make me blow a load in my pants by rubbing my cock through them.

As the table conversation dives into further boredom with a change in topic to the sensibility of leasing cars versus buying them and how the reverse is true in the real estate world, a slightly drunk Alyna leans over with her hand still on my cock and whispers the following line in my ear: "I want to go back to your place and fuck your brains out right now."

I say, "Well, ladies, it was nice to meet you. Todd, I think we should be going. We're getting kind of tired and I've got to be up early in the morning for some things."

He says, "What? What things do you have to be up early for?"

"Just some things."

"Like what? You don't have to be up early for shit."

I'm kind of buzzed and far too ready to fuck to think straight. I say, "I have to make a phone call."

This seems to confuse everyone at the table enough to allow our dismissal.

Todd says, "Oh. Well, Alyna, it was nice meeting you. I'm sure we'll be seeing more of each other around." I can't tell whether he's trying to hit on her or he's giving our burgeoning relationship a drunken vote of confidence.

She says, "Nice meeting you, too."

The fat pig and the hot bitch both say something like, "Good night, nice meeting you," but I don't care enough to actually decipher it.

As we leave I shift my hard-on to make walking more comfortable. When we get in the car Alyna says, "Jesus Christ, I thought we'd never get out of there," and she kisses me hard with a wet mouth.

When we get back to my place, she kind of pushes me down on my bed, takes my pants off, and starts sucking my cock. Without taking her mouth off my dick she somehow takes her own clothes off and maneuvers herself around into the sixty-nine position. Once again I notice her asshole smells like some kind of berry or melon and once again I enjoy it.

She sucks my dick as I eat her out, then just as I'm wondering if she's going to make good on the offer to fuck my brains out, she climbs off my face and sits on my dick. I don't really do much except lie there while she grinds on my cock.

I don't know if she can somehow sense it or if it's just lucky timing, but every time I'm about to blow a load she gets off my cock and says something like, "Fuck me doggie style," or "I want you on top."

It seems like we've been fucking for a while, but as she cums and the sound of her cumming makes me blow a gigantic load in her pussy, I look at the clock and notice that we've only been going at it for ten minutes. I wonder if she's in any way disappointed. I'm far from it. Even in the few seconds after I've expelled what must be one of the biggest loads of my life, I am fully aware that this is quite possibly the best single sexual experience I've ever had, barring maybe the first time I had my dick sucked by Jennifer Gladson my sophomore year in high school.

She lies down next to me, panting. She says, "That was amazing."

I say, "Yeah."

She doesn't really snuggle up to me, but just kind of lays a hand on my stomach and we both just look at my ceiling, breathing. The berry or melon smell from her asshole is still in my nose, which I find pleasant. I think momentarily about a conversation we had last week in which she explained that she's been on the pill since she was seventeen and it's the only form of birth control she'll use because she hates rubbers. I wonder if she was lying, or if maybe she's forgotten to take it recently and my giant load is impregnating her. Despite my overwhelming urge to ask her these questions, I remain quiet and just stare at my ceiling.

After ten or fifteen minutes pass and I'm almost asleep, I feel her hand on my dick and her lips on one of my nipples. She says, "You got another round in ya?" Judging by the speed with which my dick becomes hard, I guess I do.

chapter thirty-two

Halo 2

The next morning I wake up and Alyna's in my bed next to me, staring at me. She says, "Morning."

I say, "Good morning."

"Last night was pretty incredible."

"Yeah."

"I think we should see if we can relive a little of it this morning."

I don't know why Alyna would only suck my dick and jerk me off until last night, but apparently whatever kind of seal she had on sex has been broken. We fuck each other in a slow, controlled rhythm that makes us both cum about thirty minutes later. Then we get up, take a shower, and go into my kitchen area to look for breakfast. As we pass through the living room she notices my array of video game systems and says, "You have an Xbox 360?"

"Yeah."

"Do you have Halo 2?"

"Yeah."

"Are you any good?"

It's a strange challenge that excites me almost as much as the thought of her ass grinding against my crotch as I fuck her. We hurriedly eat two bowls of Fruity Pebbles and sit down to play Halo for the next few hours. Alyna's not the best Halo player I've ever seen and is less than a challenge for me, but I'm legitimately impressed at the level of skill she does have, and her genuine enthusiasm for the game is beyond rare for a girl.

As we play she admits to being a minor video game junkie and attributes her interest and skill to having two brothers who constantly played video games and refused to let her play shitty girl games like Tetris or Bubble Trouble when they were growing up. I want to meet her brothers.

After we play against each other on several maps and she vows that one day she'll beat me, we go online and get into a few team games. In each of them she hops in the driver's seat of the warthog and I get on the turret. She's a good driver and we do well. She says, "I love this game. I can't wait until the next one comes out."

I instantly remember a day that Casey agreed to play Halo with me. She played for a grand total of three minutes and complained that she didn't understand the controls before asking me if we could play Tetris or Dance Dance Revolution, which she later forced me to buy. When I told her that I didn't have Tetris and I didn't want to play Dance Dance Revolution because it's a shitty game, we ended up going to the Beverly Center and looking at couches in Crate and Barrel for three hours.

As the next game queues up and we can already hear the voices of some of the players who have entered the queue with us, I wonder if Alyna could ever spend three hours looking at couches.

I say, "What are your plans for the rest of the day?"

"Nothing."

The game starts and she hops in a warthog on the beach. I get on the turret.

She says, "Why?"

"I don't know, I was just wondering."

I take out a few players with a round of machine-gun fire.

She says, "Do you want to do something with me today?"

"If you want to . . . I mean, I don't want to . . ."

"Rush things?"

"Yeah."

She drives up a ramp and deposits us on the opposite side of a wall, where there are three enemy players waiting, one with a power sword. She runs him over and I take out the other two with the machine gun.

She says, "I don't want to rush things either, but if we both want to hang out with each other, then nobody's rushing anything, right?"

She spins the warthog around and we're staring down the sights of a guy with a rocket launcher.

I say, "I guess not."

We both jump off the warthog just in time to see a rocket blow it apart and both of our shields go down to half. We both whip out battle rifles and deliver a few short bursts to the rocket launcher guy's head. He goes down.

She says, "I think we should just do what feels right."

"Me too."

"Besides, I'm going to be out of town this weekend so we'll have plenty of time to not see each other."

"Where you going?"

She picks up the guy's rocket launcher and blows up an enemy player who's at a turret in the main base, then says, "I'm going back home. I haven't seen my parents at all this semester and they said they'd fly me back for a weekend because they miss me so much."

"You need a ride to the airport or anything?"

She runs out of rockets and trades her rocket launcher for a sniper rifle she finds on the ground. I slightly regret the airport offer. I don't want her to think it means more than it does.

Alyna says, "You don't have to do that."

"Don't worry about it. I'd like to do it." I have to back up my original offer.

"Okay, then yeah, I guess I need a ride."

She crouches behind a rock and waits for her shield to get back to full. I run over beside her and my cell phone starts ringing.

I say, "Dammit. Why do people always call right in the middle of a good game?"

She says, "Get it. I'll protect you." Alyna keeps playing while I answer it in the bedroom.

It's Casey. She demands that I have coffee with her as I promised and wants to know if I was ever going to call her to set it up. I explain that I've been busy and ultimately schedule our coffee date for the upcoming weekend before hanging up.

When I get back I see that Alyna's been trying to fend off enemy players from our position and my controller's vibration is evidence of this task's difficulty.

She says, "Who was it?"

"*L.A. Times* trying to sell me a newspaper subscription."

As soon as I pick my controller back up, the vibrations are replaced with stillness and my character's accompanying death grunt.

some chapter

Jenna's Picture

I'm looking through some old boxes for the Nintendo Power Glove that I got for my seventh birthday. As I take some old books from college out of a box, a picture of my old girlfriend Jenna falls out of one. It's a picture that I took of her on the beach when we went to Martha's Vineyard one summer.

I am surprised that seeing this picture makes me stop looking for the Power Glove and sit down to think about that summer and about Jenna, who I realize is now married to the shark-toothed manager of NASCAR Superstore and possibly has given birth to his shark-toothed child.

I remember that she liked to fuck outside and we fucked that summer on the beach, not far from the exact location she's standing on in the picture. I wonder if her shark-toothed husband fucks her outside. I wonder if she likes it when he jerks off in front of her. I wonder what my life would be like if she had stuck to her plan of moving to Los Angeles when she graduated. I wonder if she's fat.

In the picture she's far from it. She's wearing a bikini that accentuates her already ample C-cup tits. She's standing at an angle so her ass, which was always a little too flat for my taste, but still a great ass, looks better than I remember it. Her stomach is defined but not overly muscular.

I try to remember our first few dates and can't. For some reason I remember a specific date we had sometime in the middle of our relationship when she dragged me to a Renaissance fair and paid a fat ugly high school girl in a wench costume two dollars to kiss me. I remember her rubbing my back once when I was sick. I remember renting *The Natural* with her because she had never seen it. I remember her telling me that when she was a little kid she thought Frisbees were gas-powered.

I put the picture back in the book and put the book back in the box.

When I try to jerk off to memories of fucking Jenna I can't cum, so I spend ten minutes downloading some Internet porn and end up blowing my load to the image of a skinny, pale girl with smaller than average tits and a mole right above her pussy taking it up the ass and saying, "That's it—clean it out, clean it out."

chapter thirty-three

Coffee with Casey

I've spent almost every night with Alyna for the past week, but it surprises me that I feel something close to real sadness as I get her bag out of the back of my car and hand it to her outside the American Airlines terminal at LAX.

She kisses me. Then she hugs me and says, "Thanks for the ride, mister."

"No problem."

"I'm gonna miss you."

"I'll miss you, too."

She hugs me again, tighter this time. I feel her rock-hard tits press against me.

She says, "This is stupid. I'm only leaving for the weekend. I'll see you in a few days."

"Okay."

She gives me one more tight hug and then squeezes my ass before she says, "I'll call you from my parents' house."

"Okay."

As she walks into the terminal she blows me a kiss. I genuinely wish she was staying. I watch her ass as she walks through the sliding doors into the check-in area, then I get back in my car and leave.

I meet Casey about forty-five minutes later at the coffee shop she demanded I go to in order to prevent her from showing up at my place every night at two A.M. I'm fully prepared for a psychotic outburst.

When I walk in, she's already sitting down trying not to look too eager. She's wearing a tight shirt that shows off how decent her tits are, and since she's already sitting down, I don't get a glance at her big ass, which makes me wonder if she's somehow miraculously slimmed her ass to a normal size since we broke up. I decide to go with the odds and believe that her ass is the same size if not bigger due to dealing with the emotional stress I must have caused her.

I sit down at the table with her.

She says, "I wasn't sure you were going to come."

"I said I would."

"I know."

She takes a drink of her coffee. A group of ten or so college-age girls all wearing UCLA women's soccer sweat suits walk in. Casey notices me checking them out. I don't care.

She says, "So like let's talk."

"Okay."

"Okay."

She takes another drink of coffee, wanting me to say something. I don't want to say anything. I don't want to be sitting here. I want to be back at my apartment fucking Alyna up against my bedroom wall.

Casey says, "So . . . do you miss me at all?"

"No, I don't think so."

"What do you mean you don't think so?"

"I mean no."

"You don't miss me at all?"

"No."

She starts to tear up and I want her to cry in this coffee shop. I want to be the guy sitting across from her as she's sobbing like a stupid fucking kid right in front of the UCLA women's soccer team.

Casey says, "We were together for a year and a half and you don't miss me even a little?"

I give a little pause for impact. "Not at all."

"Are you happy?"

Even when I was with Casey, I never considered myself unhappy, but the marked difference in the amount of enjoyment that I get from my life without her in it is undeniable.

I say, "Yeah."

She says, "Happier than when you were with me?"

"Yeah."

"Why?"

The answer is clear and simple: Alyna. Alyna fucks better and more, she has an amazing ass, and she genuinely seems to like me more than the idea of being married by twenty-eight no matter what. Even though I want Casey to self-destruct right in front of me and I know telling her about Alyna will snap her like a twig, I don't.

Instead I say, "I don't know. I just am."

"Well, I don't like understand that."

"Neither do I."

"Well, if you don't understand it, then why did you break up with me?"

Casey's voice has risen loudly enough by this point in the conversation to get the attention of the soccer team, who are now poorly disguising the fact that they're listening to every word we say.

"I just had to."

"You had to?"

"Yeah."

"Why?"

"I told you I don't know."

"Can't you give us another chance?"

"No."

"I think I deserve another chance."

"I can't do that."

"Why can't you? Like what's so bad about seeing if we can work through this?"

"There's nothing so bad about it. It's just not going to happen."

"You wouldn't go out on a date with me?"

The thought of going on a date with Casey and trying to see how many holes I could put my cock in before the night ended does pique my interest, but my unyielding urge to run out the front doors of the coffee shop and never see Casey again for the rest of my life holds more weight.

I say, "No."

Casey's close to losing it. She slows down and takes a long swig of her coffee. I look at the UCLA women's soccer team and they all quickly try to look at something else. Casey also notices that they've been watching us.

She says, "Can we go back to your apartment and talk about this?"

"Why?"

"Because this is like a private conversation and I don't really want to be having it in public."

"I think we should stay here."

"Why?"

"It's better that way."

She drinks more coffee.

She says, "You know, my mom always told me she never liked you."

"You should have listened to her."

"I just can't believe you're doing this."

"It's already done."

"How can you just stop loving me?"

In possibly one of the most honest moments of my life I say, "I don't think I ever really did."

And that's the end of Casey's emotional fortitude. She starts bawling like a baby. The UCLA women's soccer team doesn't even try to conceal their voyeuristic interest in what's going on or their apparent contempt for me, judging by the scowls on their faces.

I offer nothing to Casey, no words, no hug, nothing. Instead I get up out of my chair and turn to leave. As I take my first step away from the table I decide to get in my car, which is parked across the street, and sit for the next ten minutes to watch Casey cry. But I don't get to my car. I don't even take another step before Casey pukes out the following sledgehammer to my nuts:

"I'm pregnant."

My asshole clenches so tight that I'm pretty sure I tear my sphincter.

some chapter

Milla Jovovich

She's standing right in front of me in the bread aisle at Ralph's on Sunset holding a basket half full of fingernail polish, and I watch her fill up the other side with five bags of powdered donuts. I wonder if I knocked up Milla Jovovich if she would have an abortion, but I would probably be okay with whatever Milla decided to do.

I lose any memory of the purpose of my visit to the grocery store. I'm holding a packet of superglue and a can of beef stew, both of which I reason I must have had some need for or I wouldn't have been holding them. All I can think about is jerking off to Milla Jovovich's nude scenes in *Return to the Blue Lagoon* as a teenager. I can also think about seeing her tits and cunt in *The Fifth Element* and *Resident Evil,* which I promptly do when she squats down to get another bag of powdered donuts off the bottom shelf.

I specifically key in on the scene in *Resident Evil* when she wakes up strapped to a medical examination table wearing only a piece of paper and her pussy is clearly visible. I follow her into a checkout line.

As she checks out, she uses a Ralph's card, which the computer says yields her no savings on the brands of fingernail polish and powdered donuts she chose to purchase. She pays with a credit card and asks to have her items put in a plastic bag.

I watch her ass as she walks away from the checkout counter. It's fucking perfect beyond belief.

I rush the cashier through my checkout procedure and pay in cash, carrying my beef stew and superglue out of the store without a bag to expedite my departure. I'm not sure exactly why I'm in such a hurry to watch Milla Jovovich walk to her car but I am.

I see her get into a black Escalade. I get in my own car and fail to resist the urge to follow her, which I do until I see her pull into a driveway at a house in the Hollywood Hills that looks like it must cost more than it's worth.

That night at home, I eat the beef stew and imagine what it would be like to fuck Milla Jovovich. I wonder what my unfounded odds of ever fucking her are. I give myself a 1.33 percent chance based on the following criteria: (1) I live in Los Angeles, where she must spend a significant amount of time, increasing my chance of running into her randomly; (2) she married the guy who directed *The Fifth Element*, who is a fucking toad; and (3) she is a supermodel/actress, and all of those types love to party and love to fuck.

Satisfied with my odds, I put on my *Resident Evil* DVD and jerk off to any scene that features her in little or no clothing. I blow a load but still can't remember what I bought the superglue for.

chapter thirty-four

It's Official

Over the course of about a month and a half Alyna and I have fucked enough for me to know the following things: She likes it when I spread her ass cheeks apart in doggie style and press my thumb on her asshole; she can't cum unless I talk dirty or spank her; and she loves to have me stick my cock halfway in, then jerk me off so I shoot a load in her pussy.

But as we eat Combo Burritos at the Taco Bell by the Beverly Center, I'm not thinking about any of these things. I'm thinking about the fact that Casey is fucking pregnant. I only vaguely remember the last few times we fucked, and even though I know a large percentage of those times ended with me blowing my load all over her face/ass/stomach, I do remember at least a few times that I shot my load in her cunt because she said she didn't like it when I came on her face. I shouldn't have let her manipulate me. This entire thing could have been avoided. I wonder if Alyna would care if I had a kid.

I'm chewing on a piece of Combo Burrito and thinking of ways to have Casey accidentally die when Alyna says, "If we were out somewhere and ran into some friend of yours that I haven't met, how would you introduce me?"

"I'd say . . . this is Alyna. How would you introduce me?"

"I don't know, I might say something like . . . this is my boyfriend. What do you think of that?"

I chew a piece of my burrito as I give it some thought. I say, "I wouldn't mind." Strangely, I really wouldn't.

"And you wouldn't mind if I was your girlfriend?" I wouldn't mind this, either.

I say, "No. Would you?"

"Obviously not, or I wouldn't be asking. I just felt like we see each other so much and I like you a lot and it seems like you like me just as much. . . . We might as well be official."

I search for the uneasy paranoia this conversation should be building in me, but it's not there. What is there is a strange sense of relief, which doesn't bother me as much as it should. I'm actually happy to have another girlfriend, and not because a girlfriend means free and easy fucking, but because my new girlfriend is Alyna. I almost feel like telling her about the impending life-ruining child I'm about to have with my ex-girlfriend but decide that until the kid exists it's not worth bringing up.

She says, "You don't feel weird about it being so soon after both of us just getting out of relationships?"

"No."

"Me either. Does it make you feel weird that you don't feel weird?"

"No."

"Me either."

"Does it make you feel weird that I don't feel weird?"

"No."

"I'm driving you crazy with this, right?"

"No."

"So then it's official. You're my boyfriend and I'm your girlfriend?"

"Yeah."

"Does that kind of excite you?"

As we talked I hadn't thought about it, but now that she brings it up it does kind of excite me. I've never had a girlfriend that I've found as attractive as Alyna, nor have I had one that I've wanted to spend as much time with.

She says, "You know what we should do to celebrate?"

"What?"

She says loud enough for the lady hobo sitting in the corner to hear, "We should go back to your apartment and fuck."

I've also never had a girlfriend who's wanted to have sex enough to propose it in a Taco Bell in front of a hobo.

We finish our Combo Burritos as Creed's "(Can You Take Me) Higher" starts to play on the Taco Bell radio system and the lady hobo stands up, raises her arms to the heavens, and sings along with Scott Stapp.

Back at my apartment I've been fucking Alyna up against my bedroom wall for a few minutes and I'm about to blow my load. The thought of fathering two children with different women drives me to pull out and shoot semen all over her ass and legs. As I fall back onto my bed and Alyna goes to the bathroom to clean herself up, I wonder what my kid is going to look like and wish I was dead.

chapter thirty-five

Alyna Finds My Stash

I'm sitting on the couch half watching the World Series of Poker on ESPN2. Alyna is kneeling between my legs with one hand on my balls and the other jerking me off while she sucks the head of my cock. I blow a load down her throat just as a pro poker player goes all in on a pair of aces and loses to an amateur who draws two queens on the flop to match the queen he has in the queen/ten hand he chose to stay with.

Alyna sucks my cock for a few more seconds, then says, smiling from my crotch, "Did you like that?"

"Yeah."

"I hate yeast infections because we can't have sex, but I kind of like them because I get to give you blow jobs all the time."

I wish I had never met Casey. I wish I had never fucked Casey. I wish she wasn't pregnant with the ruination of my life. Alyna says, "I'm getting a drink. You want something?"

"No. I'm good, thanks."

She walks into my kitchen area, leaving my cock hanging out of my pants. I move to start buttoning them back up and she says, "Just leave it. I want to see if I can make you cum again after I get a drink."

I wonder how difficult it would be to have Casey killed.

I watch a few more hands of the World Series of Poker. The amateur guy gets dealt the same hand—queen/ten—and goes all in again and wins again, knocking another player out of the final five. Despite having just shot a load down Alyna's throat, the thought of her wanting to suck my cock again starts to give me another hard-on.

As the next hand is being dealt, Alyna says from the kitchen, "Hey, what's this Bloussant stuff?" and I quickly realize that in the cupboard above my drinking glasses I still have half a case of unused breast-enhancing drug that I never slipped into Casey's food. I don't know what my explanation will be. The truth is probably not the best choice. As I think for a few seconds, Alyna reads one of the bottles and says, "Why do you have a breast-enhancing drug?"

I don't leave the couch. With my dick losing its semi-hard-on but still hanging out of my pants, I say, "My old girlfriend kept it over here."

"Why?"

"She didn't like to keep it at her house."

"Why not?"

"I don't know, I think she didn't want her cats to get into it." This immediately conjures images of Casey's cats walking around with gigantic tits.

Alyna comes out of the kitchen with a bottle of Bloussant in her hand and a glass of Dr Pepper in the other. She says, "Did this stuff work?"

"I don't really know."

"Do you think she'll want it back?"

"Probably not."

"Do you care if I try it?"

I wonder if there's any way on the planet that Alyna wouldn't mind the fact that I'm going to have a kid with my ex-girlfriend.

"No, go ahead."

"It can't really work, right?"

"It's supposed to."

"I have to try it."

She puts the bottle of Bloussant down on the coffee table next to her glass of Dr Pepper, then takes my cock in her hand and says, "You think you can handle another one?"

She already has her mouth on my dick when I say, "I don't know, I guess we'll have to see."

As she sucks my dick for the second time in fifteen minutes I try to picture her B-cup tits getting bigger. I put my hand down her shirt as she sucks my dick and squeeze her tits, trying to imagine them a full cup size bigger. I like her tits as they are and I'm not completely sure increasing their size would improve their overall quality, but her enthusiasm to willingly use an unproven breast enhancer is an attractive enough personality trait to make her tits somehow feel better in my hand.

The second load I blow proves to be a little too much for her mouth to handle. She swallows some of it, but some of it drips out of her mouth onto her cheek and chin and onto my dick.

She comes up from sucking my dick, laughs, and says, "Do I have anything on my face?"

As she smiles at me with my cum dripping off her chin, I can't help laughing too, partly because of the humor of the situation, but mostly to mask the utter despair I feel closing in around me when I think about the fact that the best thing I've possibly ever had is going to be destroyed by a fucking mistake that's growing in the womb of a girl I hate.

some chapter

Subway Whore

After thirty minutes of a drunken argument about the necessity and quality of the Los Angeles subway system, Todd and I find ourselves waiting at the Hollywood terminal to test it out at one A.M. Next to us a family with a retarded kid and what I assume to be some kind of junkie also wait for the next train. Todd elbows me and points in the general direction of a hobo, crouching by what I make out to be a log of human shit near the stairwell and says, "Dude, check out that guy with his deuce."

The retarded kid sees the feces at the same time Todd does and starts screaming, "Mommy, he poodied! Mommy, that man poodied on the ground!" which gets no reaction from the hobo, who remains crouched by his work. This goes on for a while.

When the subway train finally pulls up, I convince Todd to get on a car that does not contain the retarded kid, which turns out to be a mistake because the car we do get on contains a weatherworn woman who can't be any younger than fifty-five with eyes that don't really focus on anything holding a brown-stained teddy bear that at one time was pink, and a black guy in an Adidas sweat suit who I'm pretty sure is carrying at least a knife, but more likely a gun.

The train pulls away from the terminal and our fate is sealed.

Todd says, "So what do you think now?" and I'm reminded that there was an original reason for us to be on the subway.

I say, "Uh, I still think L.A. can do without it."

"Whatever, dude. This is the fucking shit."

Todd and I don't say anything for the next few minutes. Then the old lady with the bear says what I think is the following: "Kiss my bear and I'll suck your cock."

I'm positive she didn't actually say this and I'm drunk enough to say, "Excuse me?"

And she says again, "Kiss my bear and I'll suck your cock."

Todd says, "Did she just say kiss my bear and I'll suck your cock?"

The old lady says, "You bet your ass I'll suck those cocks."

Todd and I are both stunned into silence. She says again, "Kiss my bear and I'll suck your cock."

I shoot a quick glance at the black guy in the Adidas sweat suit just to see if he's getting any of this. He seems to be unfazed by what's going on and I don't know if any of this means anything to him until he says, "Well, you gonna kiss her fuckin' bear or what?" And it becomes suddenly clear to me that this man is the bear-wielding old lady's pimp. I immediately wonder if I'm going to be forced to accept a blow job from this aged and most likely disease-ridden whore at gunpoint, and worse, made to kiss her bear in order to receive the blow job.

I look at Todd, who's dazed.

I say, "Uh, no, thanks."

The pimp says, "You two faggots or somethin'?"

The old whore scratches out a laugh and then says, "Hey, faggots, you kiss my bear and I'll suck your faggot cocks."

For some reason my immediate reaction is to defend my sexuality to the pimp and his whore, so I say, "No, we're straight."

The pimp says, "Then kiss her fuckin' bear."

Todd finally chimes in, "I don't think so, man."

The whore says again, "You kiss my bear and I'll suck your cock."

The pimp says, "If you ain't gonna kiss her bear then you gotta get off this train."

I wonder how close the next stop is and hope we get to it before we're killed.

For the next five minutes the whore insists that we kiss her bear so she can suck our cocks, and the pimp keeps asking us if we're sure we're not faggots. When we get to the next stop, across the street from Universal Studios, Todd and I get off the train and make our way aboveground, where we take a cab back to the bar we originally came from in Hollywood.

As we sit back down at the bar and order two beers, Todd says, "Hey, dude, was that bitch on the subway ninety-eight percent?"

Despite the possibly life-threatening situation we managed to narrowly escape, I force myself to imagine getting head from the repulsive whore and then fucking her so I can accurately answer Todd's question.

I say, "She's about as close to a two-percenter as you can get, but if it's disease-free and she disappears right after I fuck her and her pimp's not around . . . I'd fuck her."

Todd says, "Me, too."

chapter thirty-six

Dinner with the Mother of My Child

I'm waiting outside Casey's apartment for her to come out so I can take her to a dinner she forced me to agree to, where she wants us to talk about the baby and how we're going to raise it.

When she comes out to the car she catches me a little off guard by saying, "Hey, why don't we skip the dinner, go back into my apartment, and have crazy sex?"

I'm pretty shocked by this, but even more shocked by my reaction as I say, "I think we should go eat dinner." It doesn't take me long to search for an answer as to why I passed up free grudge-fucking with my ex-girlfriend—Alyna. I don't want to cheat on Alyna. At face value, not wanting to cheat on Alyna should bother me, but as I stare at Casey I'm almost calmed by the fact that at the moment I really only want to fuck Alyna and no one else.

Casey gets in the car, puts her hand right on my dick, and says, "Then after dinner, I want you to come back here and fuck me silly." Despite the fact that Casey is carrying the doomseed of my life in her gut, this gets me pretty horny, but as soon as I get a hard-on I start thinking about Alyna and I know I don't want to fuck Casey. I'm genuinely surprised by this seemingly impregnable psychological defense I seem to have developed.

As we drive, I make sure to hit the brakes a little harder than I need to at each stop in the hopes of jarring the fetus loose and causing an instant miscarriage. As I come to the fourth or fifth abrupt stop, it doesn't seem to be working. Nonetheless, I stomp the brakes whenever traffic allows, reasoning that it only takes one good one to bust the fetus loose.

We pull into the valet at Lawry's and it doesn't seem like the fetus is detached. I walk into the place behind Casey and kick her back foot so she trips on herself going up the stairs, still hoping to jar the fetus loose. She shoots me a pissed-off look that I explain away by saying, "Sorry, it was an accident," but the unborn life-ender in her gut seems to be doing fine.

We sit down, get our water and bread, and then it starts.

She says, "So what do you think we should name it?"

I am a statue.

She says, "I was thinking Willamena for a girl and Kerry for a boy. What do you think?"

I hate both of these names. I say, "Casey, do you really think we should have this baby?"

"Uh . . . yeah. What else would we do? Give it up for adoption?"

"You could have an abortion."

"An *abortion?!?* Why would I abort a child that was conceived through love?"

"Do you remember the conversation we had in the coffee shop a few days ago?"

"Yeah, but you were just confused. You didn't know what you were saying. This baby, our baby, is going to bring us back together and make you see that you still love me, that you never stopped loving me."

I want to open the salt shaker and dump it in my eyes.

The waiter comes over and takes our orders, giving me a quick

breather from the worst conversation I've ever had in my life. Then he leaves and it's back on.

She says, "Don't you want to see what a baby that's half me and half you would grow up to be like?"

I think about this for less than a second and say, "No," with more certainty than I've ever had about anything in my life.

"But that will change once you actually see the baby. They say no man can stop himself from crying when he first sees his little baby."

"I don't want a baby. Have an abortion."

"No. I'm not having an abortion. We're having this baby and starting a family."

"What?"

"I'm sure if you just apologize to my parents and tell them you were like confused when you blew up on my mom and everything, they'll forgive you and we can still get married."

"I don't want to get married."

"Well, I'm not having a child without being married to the father."

"Then get an abortion."

"I can't believe you're being such an asshole about this."

She wants me to say something. I don't.

She says, "It was meant to be. I mean, if I was on the pill and still got pregnant, then this baby is meant to come into this world and we're meant to be its mother and father."

Now she really wants me to say something. I don't.

She says, "Well, aren't you going to say something?"

"Get an abortion."

She says, "I am not getting a fucking abortion," right as the waiter brings our drink orders to the table. He pretends he didn't hear it, but he must have. I wonder briefly if he's ever been privy to any identical dinner conversations.

She says, "We're going to get married. We're going to have this baby and we're going to start a family."

"I'm not."

"What do you mean, you're not?"

"I'm not starting a family."

"You don't have a choice. I'm going to have your baby. You're going to be a father."

"But I don't have to be around for it. All I'm required to do is pay you, which I'll do as the law dictates." I'm hoping this line of reasoning will make her realize she doesn't want to have a baby if the father won't be around.

She says, "You wouldn't want to see your child grow up?"

"No."

"Why?"

"I just don't want to."

"You wouldn't want to help me raise *our* child?"

"No."

"Why?"

"Same reason."

Our food comes. Over the course of the meal, Casey continues to try to convince me that the best thing to do is to get married, have the child, and start a family. I stand firm in my disinterest in her plans.

On the drive home I continue to try to jar the fetus loose with more abrupt driving maneuvers.

At the end of the night, she once again invites me in to have "crazy sex." Upon my refusal she reaches for my pants and says she won't take no for an answer. She explains that she's missed me and "my penis." Although I'm very tempted to fuck her just to see if a few deep thrusts might knock the fetus out of her uterus, my genuine affection and respect for what Alyna and I have keep me from leaving my car.

Once I finally get Casey to go back inside her apartment by promising to at least think about getting married, I drive to a party where I'm supposed to meet Alyna. As I drive I wonder if Alyna ever had an abortion or ever would. I assume she would but is careful enough to not get pregnant in the first place.

chapter thirty-seven

Ex-Boyfriend Duane

Other than Alyna's hippie roommate Simone, I haven't met any of her friends. Despite her telling me that she really doesn't have many friends and the party I'm at is being thrown by more of an acquaintance, I feel uneasy about the fact that I want to make a good impression, which I find even more unsettling than the party itself. I can't remember the last time I was conscious of trying to make someone happy or giving a shit about something I normally wouldn't.

As soon as I walk in Alyna takes my hand and guides me through the packed apartment. My dick brushes a couple of hard college asses as we make our way to the kitchen and a counter full of Ralph's brand hard liquor and various bottles of juice. Alyna makes herself a screwdriver and I pour myself a blue plastic cup full of scotch from a jug with a Distiller's Preference label on it and a price tag that indicates the entire gallon was a price-conscious $6.34. Even though I immensely enjoy getting drunk with Alyna, I drain the scotch in one swallow in an effort to numb the memories of my dinner with Casey and the thoughts of my bleak future.

Alyna leads me around to two girls standing by an open window. Alyna says, "Okay, I'll introduce you to these two girls. They're both complete bitches and one of them supposedly got crabs last semester from the other one when they were drunk and got dared to rub their pussies together."

Alyna introduces me.

One bitch says, "Hi. I'm Carolyn."

The other one says, "I'm Mandy."

I say, "Nice to meet you," as I'm imagining them both naked rubbing their cunts together in a drunken frenzy, which isn't bad considering they've both got late-teen bodies that haven't yet started to show the signs of wear associated with too much drinking and little to no exercise on a steady diet of eating anything they want.

The conversation I wade through yields nothing interesting aside from Alyna starting to get semi-drunk and moving her hand from the middle of my back down into my pants and pinching my ass from time to time.

As I move my hand down her pants to reciprocate, I notice she's wearing a thong. My hard-on is almost instantaneous. As I squeeze her rock-hard ass, I wonder how long it will be before she loses it, before she gets cellulite, before she becomes an old woman eating a cup of yogurt in the airport. Somewhere in the pit of my stomach the unrealistic but not entirely impossible scenario of her ass never losing its firmness and fuckability gives rise to a giddy excitement that combines with the first sip of a new plastic cup of scotch to make me feel better than I've felt in a while about anything.

The two bitches use a momentary lull in the boring conversation to announce that their drinks are empty and they have to get refills. As they leave I wonder why I was so worked up about making a good impression. A completely hot bitch who's a little taller than Alyna with slightly bigger tits comes over to talk to us, and the hope that somehow Alyna and this girl would have no problem double-teaming me is accompanied by the urge to make the best impression of my life.

The hot bitch says, "Hey, Alyna. Who's this?" in a way I interpret as indicative of her entertaining the idea of fucking me.

Alyna introduces me as her boyfriend and the hot bitch's formerly flirtatious tone changes to something closer to repulsion as she says, "I'm Brooke." I've always wanted to fuck someone named Brooke.

Brooke says, "Is he the reason you haven't been hanging out as much?"

Alyna says, "No. I mean, we've been spending a lot of time together, but I don't know. . . ."

Brooke says, "Does Duane know you have a new boyfriend?"

Who the fuck is Duane? I think he's Alyna's ex-boyfriend but I'm not sure. I am sure that I'm slowly starting to hate Brooke. As she continues to talk to Alyna like I'm not in the room, I imagine myself fucking her doggie style, pulling her head back by her hair. I imagine her crying somewhere alone. I imagine her pregnant and fat—like Casey.

Alyna says, "I don't care if Duane knows."

Brooke says, "Well, he'll find out soon enough."

And fucking Duane walks up, puts his arm around Brooke, and says, "Hey, Alyna, how's it going?" with a forced confidence and nonchalance that make him seem more drunk than he probably is.

Alyna introduces me to her ex-boyfriend.

Duane says, "Yeah, I think we met once before, but that was when I was still fucking Alyna."

Brooke laughs.

Alyna says, "Jesus Christ, this is why I fucking dumped you. You're a complete dick."

Duane misuses the phrase "That's what *she* said." Then he says to me, "So aren't you like thirty years old or something?"

Alyna answers before I can. "You know what, Duane, he's not thirty, but even if he was, it doesn't matter because I sucked his cock three times today and it stayed hard every time. So no matter how old he is, he can make me happier than you."

The fact that Alyna and I are both well on our way to being completely shit-faced helps me explain away the slight insult I feel at her reduction of our relationship to its sexual components.

At this point I've noticed that a small group of people who have obviously followed the mini-drama of Duane and Alyna in their circle of friends have gathered around us, unfortunately for him.

They watch, waiting for the rebuttal from Duane that never comes. He takes a drink from his cup and opens his mouth to say something, but instead puke comes out. His puke lands mainly on the floor and his shoes, but some of it gets on Brooke. The small crowd that's gathered around the scene disperses with the spread of Duane's cloud of vomit stink.

Alyna says, "Let's get out of here."

We leave and walk down the street to IN-N-OUT, where I buy Alyna a number one plain. We get our food and sit down.

She says, "I'm sorry about that. I didn't know he was going to be there."

"It's okay."

"I know the last thing you want to see is my asshole ex-boyfriend who's still not over it."

"Is that true about him not being able to get hard-ons?"

She kind of laughs and says, "Yeah, it is, actually."

"Why'd you stay with him so long?"

She laughs again and says, "There's more to a relationship than sex."

Hearing those words come out of her mouth scares the shit out of me for two specific and conflicting reasons. Reason 1: My earlier disappointment at Alyna's trivialization of our relationship dissolves, meaning that I actually want her to think there's something more between us than just sex. Reason 2: Casey used that exact phrase more times than I can count as an excuse to not have sex.

At the moment reason number two seems more pressing, so I say, "But that's one of the most important parts, right?"

"Oh yeah. Don't get me wrong. If I don't get sex once a day I go crazy."

"So didn't he drive you crazy?"

"Yeah. I guess it just took me a while to realize it. Why'd you stay with your girlfriend for so long?"

It's the first time anyone's asked me this and the first time I've even thought about it. It wasn't the convenience, it wasn't the boring sex, it wasn't the unemotional response I had to everything she did, it wasn't the disinterest with which I approached everything about her. As I chew my plain number one sitting across from Alyna, I pinpoint the single exact reason I stayed with Casey for a year and a half.

I say, "I guess I just didn't think there was anything better."

Alyna smiles, thinking I'm talking about her specifically as the "anything better." I don't ruin it. I smile back knowing to a large degree her smile is justified.

She says, "Do you still talk to her?"

I'm pretty sure Alyna wouldn't care if I did still talk to Casey, but fear of any conversation that could lead to my accidentally divulging the existence of my unborn child causes me to say, "No."

"When was the last time you did?"

I don't count the time she showed up on my doorstep or the time I had coffee with her and she told me she was pregnant or the time we ate dinner and I tried to convince her to have an abortion thirty minutes before I showed up to the party we just left when I say, "I don't know. Months ago."

"Do you think she's okay with everything?"

I say, "Probably."

We finish eating our number ones and then go back to my apartment, where Alyna insists on fucking in front of an open window. As we do, some people walk by on the street outside, but I don't think they notice because the lights are off.

We rest for a while and then have sex again. This time it's less aggressive, slower, with us lying side by side, and it ends with her falling asleep a few seconds after we both cum. I stay awake for a few minutes trying to imagine how pissed off Duane must have been when Alyna explained to him that she sucked my cock three times today.

I try to imagine Casey sucking some guy's cock just to see if it elicits any reaction. It doesn't. I throw in another guy fucking her doggie style while she's sucking another guy's cock. Still nothing. I think about her getting fucked in the ass and the cunt while she's sucking some other guy's dick who I imagine to be Persian. Still nothing. I end up falling asleep imagining Casey sitting in the middle of a basketball court as the entire Lakers roster surrounds her, coating her in a six-inch-thick layer of semen, and I still feel nothing except the growing paranoia created by the rising probability that the cum-drenched girl sitting center court will soon be the mother of my child.

some chapter

Gwen Stefani

No Doubt's first CD plays in Alyna's car and I still don't understand why anyone has ever bought any of their records or why Alyna and almost any girl I've ever known loves their shitty music.

This mystery remains unsolved as Alyna and I pull into the underground parking garage at the Virgin Megastore on Sunset with the intent of buying Jefferson Airplane's *Crown of Creation* because mine has been lost. As we come up the elevator and the doors open, we see a giant mob of teenage girls standing in a line that snakes around the side of the building out onto the street.

We walk into the main courtyard area of the shopping center and the crowd's source is revealed to be Gwen Stefani. She's inside the store signing copies of her various CDs, posters, and other crap.

Alyna looks at me and says, "Holy shit. I didn't know she was gonna be here. Do you mind if I go get something autographed?"

I tell her I will meet her back here and go and buy my CD, which takes me all of five minutes. I head back to meet Alyna in the mob. The line hasn't moved, and I find Alyna near the end.

The line we wait in isn't entirely unpleasant. I'm surrounded by teenage girls dressed in self-empowering belly shirts and thongs that rise up out of their pants. I wonder if the doomseed growing in Casey's gut will turn into one of these mini-bitches in fourteen years. There are a few other guys in the crowd, but I think they're fags. Alyna keeps telling me how sorry she is and how much she thinks this sucks, but I know she's enjoying it just as much as the teenage girls are. This should bother me more than it does.

The two girls directly behind us in the generally disorganized crowd that's supposed to be a line we're standing in have the following conversation:

One girl says, "I can't believe we're going to meet her."

The other one says, "I know. It's so awesome."

The other one says, "Seriously, she's like the raddest girl ever."

The other one says, "I know. I have like two posters of her."

The other one says, "Which ones?"

The other one says, "The one where she's punching all tough like and the one where she's dressed up in a pretty dress all girly."

The other one says, "I have the one where she's punching hanging over my bed."

The other one says, "Me, too."

I grab Alyna's tit over her shirt and squeeze it, which is a behavior I've gotten her used to. She turns into the squeeze, hiding it between our bodies, but not discontinuing it. But then she grabs my wrist and lowers my hand and says, "There are little kids here. Wait till we get back to your place." It's the first rejection of this type she's ever given me. I dismiss it based on the legitimacy of her argument.

I end up being forced to listen to another conversation, this one slightly more interesting than the first, between two girls who I roughly estimate to be about fifteen.

One bitch says, "Paul wants me to suck his you-know-what. Have you sucked Kenny's?"

The other bitch says, "I did it once."

The other bitch says, "What was it like?"

The other bitch says, "Kind of weird. It was totally like shoving a Blow Pop down your throat."

The other bitch says, "Did he, you know . . . finish?"

The other bitch says, "No. I had to do it with my hand."

The other bitch says, "Why didn't he?"

The other bitch says, "He said I was doing it wrong. But he hasn't even tried to go down on me, so I couldn't care less."

The other bitch says, "I don't know if I want Paul to be down in that area."

The other bitch says, "Does he ever use his hand on you?"

The other bitch says, "Yeah, sometimes."

The other bitch says, "And do you like it?"

The other bitch says, "Yeah."

The other bitch says, "Then think of how good a tongue would feel."

The other bitch says, "Yeah, I guess you're right. Maybe I should make some kind of deal with him. I'll do him if he does me."

The other bitch says, "You totally should. I think I'm going to do that to Kenny next time he wants me to suck his thing."

The other bitch says, "I can't believe we're about to see Gwen."

The other bitch says, "I know, it's so cool."

The other bitch says, "Do you think Gwen sucks Gavin's you-know-what?"

The other bitch says, "I bet she doesn't have to."

The other bitch says, "She's so awesome."

That's when I tune out and notice that even though we're still far from being next in line, Gwen Stefani is in my line of sight. She is hot as fuck. Her hard little tits are pushing out against a wife beater that has the word ROCKSTAR printed on it in rhinestones.

I imagine what she's like in the sack. My gut tells me that away from her public image, in the confines of whatever room she's being fucked in, she's completely submissive. No matter how much girl power she has, I imagine Gavin Rossdale's dick has more power. I wonder what the two girls behind us in line would think of her if they could see her with a load of Rossdale's cum sprayed all over her face.

Over the course of the next twenty minutes we make our way to the head of the line. Once there, Alyna hands her a poster she bought inside and we have the following conversation with Gwen Stefani:

Gwen Stefani says, "Hi there, who should I make this out to?"

Alyna says, "Alyna."

Gwen Stefani says, "How do you spell that?"

Alyna says, "A-L-Y-N-A."

Gwen Stefani says, "Cool name."

Alyna says, "Thanks."

Gwen Stefani signs the poster and hands it back to Alyna, then says, "There you go. Rock on."

For some reason I say, "Thanks," and we head back out into the mob.

When we get back to Alyna's apartment, she puts the poster up on her bedroom wall and fucks me like a crazed animal. I don't know if it was getting Gwen Stefani's autograph or the fact that I offered no concrete objection to waiting around to get it that got Alyna so amped up, but I don't question it.

As I look over at Gwen Stefani kicking at nothing in particular to display her unique style and empowerment, I pull out and blow a load all over Alyna's tits.

chapter thirty-eight

Two-Month Anniversary

It's been exactly two months since Alyna and I have officially referred to ourselves as boyfriend and girlfriend and in celebration we're eating at a Tex-Mex place on the coast called Marix that Alyna said was one of her favorites. I'm eating a burrito, trying not to think about my baby in Casey's stomach that Alyna still doesn't know about.

She says, "Does it seem like we've been dating for two months?"

I don't know what a good answer to this question is. I say, "No."

"I know."

I guess that was what she wanted to hear.

"So what do you think of the food here?"

"It's good."

"I'm glad you like it. I love this place."

She picks up her margarita, extends it out toward me, looks in my eyes, and says, "Let's do a toast."

I pick up my beer and clink her glass as she says, "Happy two-month anniversary."

"Happy two-month anniversary."

As what is potentially the culmination of importance in our two-month relationship is happening, Cameron Diaz walks right past our table, luring my gaze away from Alyna's eyes and making it refocus on her own unimaginably perfect body.

I stare at her for at least five or ten seconds, remembering every time I've seen her in a bikini or her underwear in a movie before realizing that I'm in the middle of my own anniversary toast. I try to turn back to Alyna as nonchalantly as I possibly can in case there is some chance to explain away my lightning-quick loss of interest in our special moment and I see that Alyna herself is staring at Cameron Diaz.

Alyna says, "God, she is so fucking hot."

Casey would have been in tears by now, questioning me about what our relationship means to me, etc.

Alyna says, "I think if I ever had sex with a woman it might be Cameron Diaz."

It takes every ounce of self-control I have not to go over to Diaz's table and ask her if she wants to have a threesome with Alyna and me. The odds obviously aren't good that she'd say yes, but lightning has to strike somewhere. I remain seated, reasoning that although I might be able to gawk at Cameron Diaz's ass on my two-month anniversary without incurring any ill feelings, I probably wouldn't be able to solicit a two-girl orgy with my girlfriend and myself.

As we finish our dinner, we both can't help taking a few more glances at Diaz, who's here with a group of friends, some of whom are guys. I try to imagine being in Cameron Diaz's circle of friends but can't because I can't get past the thought of her licking my balls while Alyna eats her out as I fuck Alyna doggie style.

About halfway through our dinner, I get up to take a piss and purposely walk too close to Diaz. She smells good.

Outside the pisser there's a guy selling flowers. I'm not worried about the possibility of not getting fucked tonight, but I decide to buy Alyna some flowers anyway, knowing it will make her happy. When I get back to the table and give them to her, I say, "Happy Anniversary."

Alyna smiles a big smile and says, "Look at you. You're the perfect little boyfriend." Then she leans across the table and gives me a kiss. As she kisses me I'm looking with one eye semi-open at Diaz, who I'm surprised to see is looking right back at our table, smiling a kind of "oh-isn't-that-cute" kind of smile. Again, I have to swallow down the impulse to invite her into a threesome.

We finish eating and I take one last look at Cameron Diaz, trying to imagine what her pussy looks like before paying the bill and going back to my apartment.

When we get inside, Alyna thanks me for the flowers and hugs me. She says, "Happy anniversary," and then kisses me and says, "Take me to the bedroom so we can have two-month-anniversary sex." I comply.

Once in the bedroom she sucks my cock a little and I eat her out some. We fuck for a few minutes and then she says, "Wait." I'm kind of scared to hear what's coming next, but when she says, "Let's do something different for our anniversary, something neither of us have ever done with anyone else," I'm interested.

She rolls over onto all fours and says, "Have you ever fucked one of your other girlfriends in the ass before?"

Of course I have, but none of them ever had an ass as rock hard and perfect as Alyna's.

I say, "No."

She says, "Neither have I, let's do it."

I can't believe I say, "You sure?"

But she erases my mistake with, "Yeah, I want to see what it's like. Do you think we need to lube up first?"

"Maybe."

We do the sixty-nine for a few minutes with me licking her asshole, which has the melon smell that I've now become familiar with. She seems to be genuinely getting off on it. This leads me to believe she may actually enjoy getting fucked in the ass, which would be something I've never experienced with another girlfriend.

After her asshole and my cock are sufficiently dripping with each other's saliva, she rolls back over onto all fours and says, "Okay, go slow at first."

As I put my cock in her asshole, she pushes her ass back toward me, forcing my dick in a few inches. The little moan she lets out isn't specific enough to let me know if she likes my dick in her ass or if it's hurting her. She pushes back again until I'm almost balls-deep in her asshole. This time the moan is accompanied by her saying, "Oh my god. That feels so good," letting me know she likes it.

I fuck her in the ass and reach around underneath her to play with her clit. Her ass is so tight I can barely move without cumming. Despite my efforts to remain totally still so as not to make myself blow an early load, Alyna keeps moving her ass back and forth, forcing my cock in and out of her.

I think about dogs getting hit by cars, my grandma, and the time I cut my knee open with the tin lid of a can of corn so deep I could see the bone. This helps me last until Alyna cums, the sound of which overcomes any repulsive or familial imagery I might be able to conjure, and I blow a massive load in her ass. As I pull out I can feel her asshole contracting around my cock. I wonder if I can get another instantaneous hard-on and start ass-fucking her again immediately. On second thought, the soreness that might result from a double inaugural ass-fucking might discourage her from ever doing it again. I pull out humbly.

As we lie in my bed she says, "Wow. That was really, really good."

"So you liked it."

"Yeah. I always thought I might, but Jesus Christ, that was almost better than normal sex. Do you like it?"

"Yeah."

"So you wouldn't care if we did that from time to time."

"Nope."

We lie there for a few minutes and then she says, "Hey, I want to tell you something and I don't want it to freak you out."

She's pregnant too, she has AIDS, she used to be a man, I have no idea what's coming as I say, "Okay . . ."

"I don't know if there's an easy way to say this so I guess I'll just say it. . . .

She's been fucking someone else. She's still fucking Duane. She's getting back together with Duane and they're getting married. Duane's in the closet with a video camera and a gun.

She says, "I'm in love with you . . . I love you."

I give in to my trained reaction and hug her, then say, "I love you, too," and I think I actually might.

"You don't have to say it back just because I did."

"I'm not just saying it back."

"You really love me?"

"Yeah," and I think I really do.

She kisses me all over the face and rolls on top of me. I wonder if my semen is going to drip out of her ass and onto me as she says, "I know this is going to sound stupid, and I don't really believe in fate or destiny or any of that stupid shit, but I kind of feel like we're meant to be together."

I don't believe in any of that shit either. Casey did. This is the first moment in our relationship that I feel slightly uneasy about how good she makes me feel. I just smile back. She hugs and kisses me again, then says, "So we're in love. Does being in love make you horny?"

She kind of grinds her cunt on my dick and it starts hardening up.

"Do you want to fuck me in the ass again?"

"If you want to."

She sits up a little and reaches back to grab my dick. Just before she inserts my cock into her ass for the second time in twenty minutes, she says, "Happy anniversary, I love you," and I wish Casey would have been into ass fucking on the night I impregnated her.

chapter thirty-nine

Another Chance Encounter

Alyna and I are in the Beverly Center because she thinks the Bloussant is working and wants to see if a C-cup swimsuit will fit her. We're holding hands as we walk into a store called Everything But Water and I'm ready to spend up to thirty minutes staring at Alyna's tits as she tries on different bathing suits, but instead I get one mind-shattering second of staring Casey right in the eye as she looks up from a swimsuit rack to see Alyna and me walking toward her.

Casey doesn't waste any time with pleasantries. She says, "Who's this?"

I'm too stunned to speak. I wonder what the odds are of a terrorist attack on the Beverly Center occurring right now.

Alyna takes over. She says, "I'm Alyna, his girlfriend. I think we met once before. I think it was actually in the Beverly Center, too."

Casey says, "His girlfriend, huh?" She shoots me a look. "Yeah, I remember that. That was like back when we were engaged. So what are you up to?"

I think she's talking to me so I respond, "Nothing."

Casey looks at Alyna and says, "So what do you do, Alyna the girlfriend?"

Alyna says, "Oh, I'm a senior at UCLA."

Casey says, "Wow, you must be all of eighteen years old."

I say, "She's twenty-one."

Casey says, "That's just great. So what are you going to do when you graduate?"

Alyna says, "I don't know yet. I haven't really given it much thought."

Casey says, "Well, good luck with that."

We all stare at one another for a few awkward seconds, then Alyna says, "Look, I'm going to go try on a few suits. You guys should catch up."

Casey says, "Yeah, we should catch up . . . because we haven't talked to each other in such a long, long time."

Alyna says, "Nice meeting you again," then heads off to the back of the store, out of earshot.

Casey looks like she wants to kill me. She says, "A *girlfriend?* I'm guessing she doesn't know that you're going to be a dad, right?"

I shake my head.

Casey says, "A fucking girlfriend?!? And she's twenty-one. We're going to have a baby. How could you get a twenty-one-year-old girlfriend?"

"I like her."

"Do you love her?"

The only thing I want to do less than have Alyna find out about my unborn child is have a conversation about my feelings for Alyna with Casey. I shrug my shoulders.

Casey says, "That means you don't. Look, I don't want to make like a big scene, so here's what you're going to do. You're going to break up with that little slut. Then next Sunday, my mom's going to be in town. You're going to go out to dinner with us and apologize to her for the last time she was out here and you're going to tell her that everything is fine between us and that we're going to get married just like we planned."

"No, I'm not."

"Then your new little girlfriend is going to find out that you're about to be a daddy."

I'm too scared to think it through rationally. I'm too horrified by the entire situation to realize that I could lie to Casey now, not break up with Alyna, and figure out something else later. I'm too terrified of letting Casey get her way and too filled with rage to think straight.

I say, "Fuck you."

Casey says, "Have it your way."

As if on cue, Alyna walks up from the back of the store with a bathing suit in her hand. Casey looks at me and musters up all of her Groundlings training as she says, "You bastard. I can't believe you didn't tell her that I'm pregnant with your child." Then she slaps me and walks off into the mall, leaving me to stare into Alyna's eyes, which tell me she's already questioning every minute of our relationship.

Alyna says, "Is that true? Did you knock her up?"

I want to lie, but not to Alyna. I say, "Yeah."

Alyna says, "That fucking sucks."

"I know."

"Will she get an abortion?"

"I don't think so."

"Fuck. That really fucking sucks."

She stands there and repeats, "That fucking sucks," a few more times, not in reaction to my life being ruined but in reaction to a relationship that could have been something really amazing getting flushed down the shitter right in front of her.

In the car on the way back to her apartment, she says that she really has fallen in love with me, but she can't deal with a kid being thrown into the picture. She breaks up with me. Luckily she's too distraught at the thought of our relationship ending to realize the logistics of

Casey's pregnancy and my knowledge of it mean that I have been in contact with her beyond anything I've ever admitted.

When we get to her apartment, she hugs me and kisses me and says good-bye. I think about telling Alyna that I don't love Casey and I don't want anything to do with the baby in her gut. But the entire situation seems too far beyond repair. There's no point.

As she gets out of the car, she cries a few tears and says, "This really fucking sucks," one more time.

As I watch her go up the stairs to her building, my sadness at the loss of Alyna turns quickly to unbridled rage for the cunt who took her away from me.

chapter forty

Carlos's Gay Party

I walk into a party with Carlos that he invited me to when I told him that Alyna broke up with me because I got Casey pregnant. The first thing I notice is that there are no women at this party.

I say, "Is this a gay thing?"

Carlos says, "Of course. What kind of parties do you think I go to?"

"Why'd you invite me to a gay party?"

"It's better than staying home by yourself."

"No, it's not."

"Well, maybe you'll meet a cute boy who'll give you a blow job and make you realize how stupid you were to ever stick your dick in a pair of meat curtains in the first place."

Then Carlos says, "I'm going to go mingle," and abandons me in the middle of an apartment full of fags.

As I go to the fridge to get a drink I run into a guy who says, "So you're here with Carlos, huh? I didn't think he had it in him."

"Excuse me?"

"To get somebody as hot as you."

"We're just friends."

"Oh, I know. I'm just friends with every guy I've ever let fuck me in the ass, too."

"I'm straight."

"What?"

"I'm straight."

The gay guy says, "Then why'd you come to this party?"

"Carlos invited me."

"Yeah, but he told you we all suck each other off at the end of the night, right?"

I'm thrown into a catatonic state by the impact of the guy's statement. Then he squeezes my arm and says, "Just kidding," followed by a gay laugh.

He says, "We fuck each other in the ass . . . just kidding again. But he did tell you this was like an all-gay party, right?"

"No."

"That little shit."

Carlos comes back from wherever he was. He says, "Tedward, you better not be trying to suck my friend's dick. He's straight."

Tedward says, "I know, that's what he said. Why'd you bring him here?"

Carlos says, "He told me he didn't have anything to do tonight. His girlfriend dumped him because he got his ex-girlfriend pregnant."

Tedward says, "I'm so glad I'm a fag. I couldn't handle some whore telling me she was pregnant and not really knowing the truth."

It has never really occurred to me that Casey could be lying. I say, "What do you mean not knowing the truth?"

Tedward says, "Women lie constantly to get their way. They can be seriously bitter cunts. At least with a guy you always know they want to fuck and you always know they're not pregnant."

Carlos says, "He's right. I fucking hate deceitful bitches. You know you should find out if Casey really is pregnant before you go throwing your life away and marry her or some stupid shit."

I say, "How do I do that?"

Carlos says, "Get one of those home pregnancy kits and make her pee in it."

I say, "She's not going to agree to take a home pregnancy test."

Carlos says, "You'll figure out some way to do it if you really think she might be lying."

Tedward says, "As enthralling as this conversation about cunts is, I must conclude my participation in it. It was nice to meet you"—he shakes my hand—"but I'm off to find a cock to suck." Then he moves off into the crowd.

Carlos says, "He's an even bigger slut than I am, and that's saying something."

I say, "Do you really think she could be lying?"

Carlos says, "Does a cunt smell like rotten fish?"

There is something comforting about the possible hope this suspicion has created in me. I don't want to talk about it anymore for fear I might change my mind and accept her declaration of pregnancy as fact when I now know some doubt exists. I want the doubt.

I say, "So why didn't you tell me this was an all-gay party?"

"If I did, would you have come?"

"No."

"Exactly. But now that you are here, drink your drink and be my wingman."

"You want me to help you pick up gay guys?"

"Of course. Why do you think I invited you? Fags are attracted to straight guys like moths to flame. All you have to do is just stand here and get hit on, then when you tell them you're straight they'll have to talk to me."

"Jesus Christ." I'm gay bait.

"Just shut up and do it, here comes our first victim."

A gay guy comes up to me and says, "I'm Jim. You've got a great ass."

I can't even begin small talk. I just say, "I'm straight."

Jim says, "Hey, man, I wasn't hitting on you, I was just saying you've got a great ass."

Carlos jumps in, "How is that not hitting on somebody? And what about my ass?"

Jim says, "Are you straight, too?"

Carlos says, "Nope."

Jim looks at Carlos's ass and says, "Eh, your straight friend's ass is better."

Carlos says, "Fuck you. How dare you."

Jim ignores Carlos and says to me, "So you're straight, huh?"

I say, "Yeah."

Jim says, "You ever wonder what it'd be like to have your cock sucked by a guy?"

I say, "Nope, sorry."

Carlos jumps back in, "Oh, and you're a fucking bottom?"

Jim says, "Yeah, so?"

Carlos says, "So get the fuck out of here."

Jim says, "Fine," and walks off back into the party.

The same scenario plays itself out at least a dozen times, with Carlos getting a couple of phone numbers and ultimately blowing some guy in a back bedroom while I deflect gay advances for twenty minutes. When he comes out of the bedroom with the guy he just blew, he says, "I told you it would work."

After the party I go back to my apartment with a new sense of the possible future—one in which Casey does not have my seed growing in her womb, one in which Alyna and I are together, one in which I still have no idea how to secretly administer a home pregnancy test to Casey.

As I close my eyes and reflexively start going through a mental list of things that I hate about Casey, I stop on one item—she never flushes the toilet after she takes a piss.

some chapter

Finger in the Two-Hole

Todd and I are at Barney's Beanery after work. He's been staring at the same bitch for the past thirty minutes, assuring me that as soon as she notices him looking at her, she'll come over and talk to him. She's looked directly at him multiple times and has made no movement in this direction.

I say, "It might help if you weren't leering at her."

He says, "Dude, you gotta let 'em know what you want. I don't want her coming over here asking me for my phone number. I want her coming over here asking me to suck my dick. And P.S., dude, I don't really need advice on picking up women from the guy who fucking locked himself into eighteen years of prison with a bitch he doesn't even like."

"It's not my choice at this point."

He says, "Whatever, dude. Okay, fuck this shit."

He walks over to the girl and her two friends and somehow gets them to come over and sit at our table.

I don't remember any of their names even as they say them, and nothing any of them says holds even the most remote amount of interest for me, until one of the girls who is moderately attractive and not too fat launches into the following story:

"I work for this catering company that does big events for famous people and movie openings and things like that. And this one time we were doing a private party at Joel Silver's house. And I was walking around serving drinks and everything. And Bruce Willis and Mel Gibson and all of these crazy famous people were there. And it was completely surreal. And so I'm handing a drink to Keanu when I hear this weird voice behind me go, 'Come here, I want to show you something.' And I turn around and it's this huge '80s movie star. And he's going, 'Come back here, I want to show you something amazing.' And he takes me by the arm and kind of starts pulling me back toward the pool house. And so I go, 'I have to work. I can't really leave.' And he goes, 'It's okay, you're with me.' And his wife is completely watching the whole thing go down, but he's still pulling on my arm, going, 'Just come with me for a few seconds.' And so I finally just go, 'I really can't, I'll lose my job.' And he goes, 'Okay, then just go into the bathroom, stick your finger up your asshole, and then come out here and let me smell it.' And I couldn't believe it."

She keeps talking, but I think I got the only important information in what turns out to be a story that lasts for ten more minutes about how many crab cakes Chris Rock ate. I wonder if her story is true.

I wonder what the storyteller's asshole smells like. I wonder if it smells as good as Alyna's.

chapter forty-one

The Test

I have done more preparation for this night than possibly any other in my life. I have purchased a home pregnancy kit. I have agreed to meet Casey and her mother for dinner but insisted on picking them up at her apartment before we leave, knowing that I'll be invited in for a few minutes and Casey will piss before we leave, as is her habit, and that she will not flush the toilet, as is also her habit. I have invited Alyna to meet me at the bar of the restaurant in which I will be dining with Casey and her mother. She doesn't know that Casey and her mother will be there and assumes that I just wanted to have dinner with her to talk about how things ended. I am hoping to surprise her by publicly unveiling the possible truth about my pending fatherhood. I have rehearsed the "I know you're not pregnant and here's the proof" speech, making slight dramatic alterations to increase the amount of emotional duress I can cause both Casey and her mother without making Alyna think I'm a psychotic monster. I have done all of this as I pull up to Casey's apartment with the home pregnancy kit tucked away inside my jacket.

I knock on her door, which is opened by her mother, who offers me a hug unprompted. I do not hug her back. As she presses her small and shriveled tits against me, she says, "Casey explained everything. You were just confused. I understand this is a big decision and it's better that you came back to it after having doubts. It only makes your bond that much stronger. Luckily we can salvage some of the initial wedding planning we did."

I offer nothing in response. As she lets go of me I hope more than I've ever hoped for anything that in a few hours I'll be able to crush her soul one more time.

Casey comes out of her bedroom with a giant smile on her face, oblivious to the sledgehammer I hope to deliver to her psyche tonight.

She says, "Well, are we ready to get going?" and it seems completely possible that she's going to walk out the door without peeing.

I'm about to ask her if she needs to pee when she says, "Just let me use the ladies' room and then I'll be ready."

As Casey pisses, I can almost feel the home pregnancy kit getting warmer in my jacket pocket. Her mom says, "You should probably wait to apologize to me until we're at dinner, you know, so it can be just right and so Casey can hear it, too. I think she'd like that."

I say, "Okay." I can hear Casey washing her hands in the bathroom as I stare at her mom, imagining myself waving the negative pregnancy test result in her face, telling her to fuck off and walking out with Alyna.

When she comes out I say, "I think I need to use the restroom, too. I'll be right back."

Casey says, "Hurry, the reservations are in twenty minutes," as I shut the bathroom door behind me.

I walk to the toilet bowl and lift the lid. There below me in all its golden glory is a bowl full of Casey's just-squirted piss. I pull out the home pregnancy kit. The directions require the possibly pregnant woman to hold the end of the strip in her urine stream for three to five seconds.

I dip the strip in the toilet for three to five seconds. The directions further require you to wait for seven minutes while the chemical effect takes place, producing either a blue or a pink result. Over the course of the next seven minutes, I'm sure Casey will knock on the bathroom door to ask me what's taking so long. Instead I hear her ask her mom the same question and her mom actually cuts me some slack by saying, "Leave him alone. He's probably nervous about this whole thing and he's having some bowel trouble."

At the end of seven minutes, the strip is neither pink nor blue, but instead the same tan color it was when I pulled it out of the box. Further examination of the directions reveals the following line:

Grip the strip firmly while urinating. If the strip is accidentally dropped into the toilet bowl, the test's results should be considered invalid as water will dilute the necessary chemical reaction.

Fuck.

Realizing there's no place I can safely dispose of the strip or the box in Casey's bathroom without leaving a clue to my clandestine pregnancy test, I wash the strip off, put it back in the box, and put the box back in my jacket pocket, hoping that I don't smell like piss. Then again, if I do smell like piss, maybe it will make the night even worse for Casey and her mom.

I leave the bathroom and we all get in my car to drive to the restaurant, where Alyna is going to meet me at the bar and my plan is going to fall apart miserably.

We walk into the restaurant, Lala's, one of Casey's favorites, and I don't see Alyna at the bar, which is small enough for me to conclude that she is not here yet. We take our seats at a table near the bar. We get bread and water, and Casey's mom starts in immediately.

She says, "So, now that we're all here and sitting down to a nice dinner and everything is happening like it was supposed to . . . do you have something to say?"

I'm on the verge of sweating visibly as I think about how Alyna is going to react to this whole thing and about whether Casey is actually pregnant. I don't say anything. Casey nudges me.

I say, "Uh, yeah. I, uh, I'm sorry for everything that happened last time you were out here."

Her mom says, "Well, that wasn't very heartfelt."

My heart is about to jump out my fucking throat. All I can picture is Alyna crying when she sees me with Casey and her mom and I can offer no explanation for inviting her here to meet me.

I apologize for the apology. "Sorry."

Her mom says, "Listen, it took a lot for me to accept the idea that you were getting back together. I mean, don't get me wrong, I like the idea of Casey getting married a lot more than I like the idea of her having to spend another year looking for another husband, but you seem a little ungrateful for my forgiveness."

I'm momentarily jarred out of my paranoia by a quick shot of hate. I want to tell her mom to fuck off, but it's not part of the plan, even though the plan doesn't exist anymore. Every time someone walks through the front door, I know it's one person closer to being Alyna and one second closer to being the last time I ever see her again.

I apologize again. "I'm sorry." It's all I can say.

Her mom says, "That's fine, I guess."

Casey says, "Good. Now that that's out of the way, let's talk about the wedding. We should have it in a few months, I think—just like we had planned."

Her mom says, "I agree. No sense in letting the planning we've already done go to waste."

I can't sit at the table anymore. I have to leave. I have to think, somehow salvage my plan.

I say, "'Scuse me. I have to go to the bathroom," then leave the table without bothering to look at their reaction.

In the bathroom I pull out the pregnancy test, hoping against all hope that it has changed to some discernible color. No luck, still fucking tan. A guy is taking a massive shit in one of the stalls. Still, the smell of his deuce is preferable to the company of Casey and her mom.

I wash my hands and think about a few ways out of this:

1. Climb out the window.
2. Fake a stroke.
3. Force myself to shit my pants so we all have to leave before Alyna gets here, which should be any second.
4. Throw myself in front of a bus.

And then it hits me—I can just go on with my plan. I may not have the concrete evidence to back up a nonpregnancy accusation, but I might not need it. The accusation alone might be enough to bring out the truth. I'll have to sell it, and once I go down that road I won't be able to turn back. But I really have no other choice. Worst-case scenario—I'm still the father of Casey's unborn child and her mom still hates me. Nothing lost, really.

I rinse my hands off, splash a little water on my face, and prepare to initiate a public scene.

As I walk out of the bathroom, I see Alyna sitting at the bar. She says, "Hi," with sadness.

I say, "Hi. Watch this and no matter what happens, don't leave."

I don't give her a chance to respond before I walk up to Casey and her mom, pull out the pregnancy test, and say loudly enough for most of the tables in the place to hear, "Casey, I know you're not pregnant."

I've never seen someone's face when their heart explodes, but I'm pretty sure that's what I'm looking at as Casey's mom falls out of her chair and her mouth and eyes get big enough to make her look like a cartoon.

I keep going, "When you pissed at your house, I did a little test and it came back negative."

Casey's mom looks at Casey and says, "Pregnant?" in a way that makes me realize Casey never told her, which gives more weight to my current paper-thin argument.

The whole place is stunned into silence. No waiters or managers are telling us to shut up. No one is saying shit. They're all just watching us.

Casey says, "Mom, I was going to tell you after we were married," which takes my argument back down a notch.

Nonetheless, my course of action is set. I continue on with, "Casey, you're not pregnant, I have the results right here."

Casey looks at her mom lying on the ground, panting and heaving like someone shot her, then she looks back at me, like she's deciding something. Then she says, "I am pregnant. Your test must be wrong."

There's no turning back. I say, "These things are ninety-nine-point-nine percent accurate," having no real idea how accurate they are. "Do you think you're the point-one percent that the test failed on? Not likely."

From the ground her mom says, "I can't believe you had premarital sex. Oh my god. Your father is going to be so disappointed in you."

The line about her dad does something visible to Casey, who starts to cry. It physically hits her, changing the look on her face from wrongly accused innocent pregnant girl to Daddy's biggest disappointment.

Casey says, "Fine. I'm not pregnant."

Holy motherfucking shit. With those three words, Casey releases me from a prison that never existed in the first place. I'm washed over with an immediate and palpable sense of euphoria, like I just woke up with a hard-on after having a nightmare that my dick got cut off.

As Casey admits her lie, I look across the room at Alyna for the first time. She has a weird look on her face. I can't tell if she's happy or horrified. I turn back to Casey, who is now helping her mom back up to her feet, and toss the pregnancy test at her. I want to say something really cool or really mean to drive a nail into her coffin, but instead I say, "Here," and walk over to the bar where Alyna's sitting, grab her hand, and walk out the door.

On the street Alyna says, "So I guess you didn't really just invite me out for drinks."

"No."

"That was fucking insane, by the way."

"Are you mad at me?"

"Mad? No. I'm happy. For the past week I haven't been able to eat. I haven't been able to sleep. I haven't been able to do anything except think about the possibility that I might never see you again and you'd be stuck in some shitty life raising a kid you don't want with a girl you don't love."

What I feel for Alyna as I hear her say this is more than affection, more than respect. It's unquestionably love.

She puts her arms around me, kisses me, and says, "Why did you invite me here to see all this, though? You could have just told me you found out she wasn't pregnant."

"I didn't want you to question it, I guess."

"Well, you accomplished that goal."

"So what do we do now?"

"Pick up where we left off. But what about your ex-girlfriend and her mom?"

"Fuck 'em."

As Alyna and I walk to my car, I don't think about what's happening inside the restaurant. I don't think about Casey's world being shattered. I don't think about how she and her mom are going to get home. I think about Alyna, her perfect ass, her lips around my cock and fucking her doggie style as I press on her asshole with my thumb. And more than that, I think about waking up with her tomorrow morning.

some chapter

Hot Girls Give Gay Guys Partial Handjobs

I'm at a bar with Todd. He's drunk and reacting to the story about Casey being forced to admit that she wasn't pregnant.

He says, "Holy shit, dude, that is some good-ass shit. It makes sense, too, that one night she was all over you, trying to suck your cock and shit in the car. She wanted you to fucking drop some seed in her hole so she could get pregnant and make her lie true. Dude, you're fucking lucky to be done with that crazy bitch. Here's to being done with crazy bitches."

He raises the pitcher of beer he's drinking from and we toast to being done with crazy bitches.

He nods in the direction of a girl and her less attractive friend in our vicinity and says, "See that hot bitch over there?"

I say, "Yeah."

Todd says, "I wanna try out a new technique I read about on the Internet. But I need your help."

I say, "What do I have to do?"

Todd says, "Pretend I'm gay."

I say, "What?"

Todd says, "Dude, just do it," and then walks over to the girls, points at me, and says with an overly affected gay lisp, "See my friend over there? We have a bet and I was wondering if you guys would come over and help us settle it."

Hot girl says, "Sure."

Less attractive girl says, "Okay," and they both come over.

Todd says, "So here's the deal. I'm gay."

Hot girl says, "Okay," just as confused as I am by this point.

Todd says, "My friend here seems to think that no man is 'too gay' to be aroused by a hot woman, which we have a ten-dollar wager on. Now I know this is a weird request, but to help us settle the bet, I was wondering if you'd be interested in trying to, you know, arouse me."

Even as I hear the words come out of his mouth, I can't believe he's saying them. I've known Todd to use some extreme measures in the past, but this is by far the most insane I've ever seen him. I'm ready to witness a drink getting thrown in his face, a slap, a bouncer tossing him out when she starts screaming rape, but instead she smiles and says, "And you're gay, right?"

Todd says, "Queer as a three-dollar bill, honey," with his thickest gay lisp yet.

She says, "All I have to do is get you hard?"

Less attractive girl says, "This is nuts," but in an encouraging way.

Todd says, "You won't be able to, but yeah, that's the bet."

She says, "And I can do anything I want to you?"

Todd says, "Well, within reason. I mean, we are in a bar here."

She gives her drink to her friend and says, "Okay."

What I witness in the minutes that follow makes me want to cry.

She puts her hand under Todd's shirt and bites his ear, then takes a step back and looks at him.

Todd says, "Nothing."

She gives him a fourteen-second tongue kiss while pressing her B cups against him, then steps back and looks at his crotch, which gives no conclusive proof one way or the other.

Todd says, "Still nothing."

She says, "Are you sure? Not even a little bit?"

Todd says, "Limp as a noodle."

She musters up her strength for one more attack. She leans in close to Todd's ear, whispers something, and then puts her hand down the front of his pants and starts jerking him off right in front of me and her less attractive friend, who seems to be more entertained by the show than even Todd is as she says, "Yeah, get that thing," and takes another drink of her Long Island iced tea.

After what I estimate to be a minute and a half of solid tugging at Todd's cock with the hot girl saying, "It feels hard, is that it?" and Todd saying things like, "It's not totally hard. That doesn't really count," she finally says, "That's a hard-on," and pulls her hand out of Todd's pants.

The hot girl then puts her hands in the air in victory and says something like, "Whoo-hooo! I gave a fag a boner," then to me, "Looks like you win ten bucks."

Later that night at Alyna's apartment, she refuses to believe me as I recount the night's events to her, which sound too fantastical to be real even to me as I say them. Her main problem with the story's plausibility is Todd's ability to suppress an erection when a hot girl is kissing him and rubbing his chest and eventually jerking him off for well over a minute.

I offer that the girl might have been drunk enough to take Todd's word that he didn't have a full erection or Todd might actually have some kind of superhuman erection-suppressing ability.

Alyna asks me how long I think I could suppress a hard-on if a hot girl was tugging at my cock. She then gives me a hand job and I suppress my erection for twelve seconds.

chapter forty-two

Casey's Underwear

I keep most of my pornographic videocassettes and DVDs in the living room with the rest of my home video collection. But there are a few choice DVDs that I keep in my bedroom closet for quick viewing on the DVD player in my bedroom. This is what I tell Alyna after she asks me if I have any porn because she wants to watch one with me and do everything they do in the movie.

As she goes into my closet, I hope she picks out *Cream Queens 3* so we can reenact the scene in which a bitch puts a popsicle in her cunt and then eats it. Then I realize that I don't have any popsicles and decide to hope for her to choose *Tit Bangers* because I've only titty-fucked her a few times and I wouldn't mind doing it again.

As she says, "Hey, what's this?" I'm already forming my explanation for the *Teeny Weenies* DVD given to me as a gag gift, which I left in the closet along with the box of lube Todd packed with it for my twenty-fifth birthday. But to my surprise she's holding up a pair of Casey's old underwear.

I say, "I think those are a pair of my ex-girlfriend's underwear."

"Why do you still have them?"

"I don't know. They must've gotten thrown in there at some point and she never got them back."

Despite the fact that this explanation is probably exactly true, I don't think Alyna buys it.

She says with a malicious smile on her face, "You don't take them out from time to time and sniff them?"

"No."

The sight of Alyna standing at the foot of my bed completely naked holding Casey's underwear is strange, but even stranger is the sight of Alyna putting on Casey's underwear, which she does.

"These are kind of big."

"She had a big ass."

"Do you like big asses?"

"I like your ass."

"Do I have a big ass?"

"You have a perfect ass."

She walks around my bedroom in Casey's underwear.

She says, "I want you to show me how you fucked her."

"I don't really want to do that."

"Why not? Did you guys do some seriously weird shit?"

"Not as weird as this."

She gets on top of me with her back to me and grinds her ass on my cock.

She says, "Did you like it when she'd do this? Did you like her big ass on your dick?"

I actually kind of did like her ass on my dick, but it was rare that she'd put it to use in our sexual encounters. As I look at Alyna's ass in Casey's underwear I start to become painfully aware of the fact that the underwear fits Alyna a little too well. By no means does she fill them out like Casey did, but neither are they grossly oversized on her.

This semi-alarms me, but I convince myself that it's some trick of my mind brought on by the mental overload created by seeing my current girlfriend in my old girlfriend's underwear.

Feeling that my dick has become hard enough for insertion, Alyna reaches down, moves the part of Casey's underwear covering her pussy to the side, and guides my cock into her. As she rides me, she looks back occasionally and smiles a weird kind of smile that I don't know quite how to take. But when her head is turned away from me and all I see is her ass in Casey's underwear bobbing up and down on my cock, I try as hard as I can to imagine that I'm really fucking Casey.

When I reach out and actually touch Alyna's hard little ass as she rides my dick, the illusion is broken, but for the most part I do a good enough job that I might as well be fucking Casey.

I blow my load to the memory of fucking Casey doggie style on a hot summer afternoon when she was drenched in sweat from jogging.

chapter forty-three

Cap and Gown

In two weeks Alyna will graduate with a bachelor's degree in film studies from UCLA. This never crosses my mind as she's sucking my cock an hour before we're supposed to go pick up her cap and gown at the UCLA bookstore.

The blow job started with me asking her to suck my cock, which doesn't strike me as out of the ordinary until I realize I've never had to ask before. This realization would bother me significantly if it wasn't immediately overshadowed by something I find vastly more important and disturbing as I blow my load—she does not swallow. Not only does she not swallow, but she doesn't even let me finish in her mouth. Instead, as I'm about to cum, she takes my dick out of her mouth and jerks me off in a dozen or so quick strokes that send streams of my semen all over her hands and my dick and balls.

Although she's never done this before and I much prefer her normal technique of swallowing my cum and then sucking my cock for roughly thirty postejaculatory seconds in order to rid my dick of any semen that might not have gone down her throat initially, I have no intention of bringing it up with her until she says, "Oooh, you made a mess."

I have to say, "No, you made a mess."

"Hey, I got you off, didn't I?"

"Yeah, but you usually swallow."

"I know."

In the least accusatory tone I can muster, I say, "So why didn't you?"

She says, "I don't know. I just didn't feel like it."

There are four explanations I can conjure for what she just said: (1) She's fucking somebody else whose semen she's more interested in swallowing than my own; (2) she's lost her taste for semen altogether, which seems unlikely based on several months of evidence to the contrary; (3) she just didn't want to do it before she gets her cap and gown, which makes no sense but seems plausible for a girl; or (4) she's lost her will to suck dick, which is a more serious issue and one I'm not willing to entertain.

I accept her answer at face value and walk to my bathroom to mop up my seed with toilet paper, which takes me longer to get out of my pubic hair than I would have imagined.

When we get to the bookstore, there are roughly seventy-five to a hundred other students also there to get their caps and gowns. I overhear some of the following dialogue:

"I have a few interviews lined up, but nothing that I'm really excited about." . . . "Yeah, we'll probably get engaged over the summer and then start looking for a house next year after we've saved up some money." . . . "Dude, I don't give a fuck. Tell him I'll pay for two kegs and he can pick up the other two. . . . "I don't know, I've been thinking about going to grad school." . . . "Moving in with my parents." . . . "My uncle has a houseboat he said I could live on for a while."

As Alyna and I approach the table where a fat bitch wearing glasses sits sorting through cap and gown orders, a semi-hot bitch wearing gym attire stops us with, "Hey, Alyna."

Alyna says, "Hey, Jenny," then introduces us and explains that Jenny was her freshman year roommate. Judging from Alyna's response to her greeting I don't think they've talked much since freshman year.

Jenny says, "So can you believe we're graduating?"

Alyna says only semi-patronizingly, "It's pretty crazy."

Jenny doesn't catch it. She says, "I know. I thought I was gonna be here for freaking ever." Then she asks me, "Are you graduating this year, too?"

I say, "No," and wonder if I really look enough like a college student to warrant that question from her.

Jenny says, "So what're your plans after the big day?"

Alyna says, "I don't know. My parents are coming out here . . . ," which is something I remember she told me about a few days ago but I had forgotten until now. She continues, ". . . We'll probably go out and eat or something."

Jenny laughs. "No, silly, I mean what are you going to do with your life? Do you have a job lined up or anything?"

Alyna says, "No, we haven't really figured out what we're going to do yet," and they keep talking but the word "we" is ringing so loud in my ears that I can't hear what else they say.

It's true "we've" never talked about what "we're" going to do after graduation, but "I'm" not going to do anything significantly different from what "I'm" currently doing, which is wish I was fucking Alyna instead of listening to her talk to this bitch who has somehow posed a question that elicited the "we" response from her.

I don't particularly dislike the fact that she used the term "we" when talking about the possible direction of her future, but I'm far from being comfortable with it. I wonder how much further down the road she has thought about our relationship beyond the next time we're going to fuck.

The ringing dies down in time for me to hear Jenny say, "Well, good luck," and although this wish of good fortune most likely has nothing to do with me, I wonder if the part of the conversation I missed included Alyna detailing her plan to somehow force me into marriage.

Jenny leaves, we pick up Alyna's cap and gown, and just as we're leaving the bookstore she says, "What do you think we should do?"

I say, "I think we should go back to my apartment and fuck."

She says, "I mean when I graduate."

I say, "I think you should do whatever you want to."

We don't talk any more about it as we walk back to my apartment, where I steer our foreplay in the direction of a blow job and contemplate attempting to see if Alyna will refuse to swallow my load again, but my urge to fuck her in the ass wins out and she cums bent over a chair as I hold one of her legs up in the air and ram my cock into her ass a little harder than I think I ever have before.

some chapter

Scarface Part 3

I'm in the Beverly Center looking for something to wear to Alyna's graduation. I go into Banana Republic and find a decent pair of pants and a shirt.

I walk up to the counter to pay, but nobody's there to complete the transaction. A gay guy walks by and says, "Is someone helping you?"

I say, "No."

He gets on a telephone and makes the following storewide page: "Amy to the front register, Amy to the front register." Then he says, "Someone will be right with you," and disappears somewhere in the back instead of selling me the clothes himself.

When Amy comes to the register I almost shit my pants. Amy is Scarface, who I haven't dealt with since she last called me and I rejected her offer to take me on a date. In the light of day I notice that Scarface has a hot little body, but her hairlip is more repulsive than I remember.

I'm not positive she remembers me as I toss my shit down on the counter in front of her, but when she says, "So how've you been?" I'm pretty sure she knows exactly who I am.

I have to say, "Fine. You?"

"Oh, pretty good. You know, just working."

I wonder what Scarface is like in the sack as she slides my credit card through the machine. I imagine she would let me do anything I wanted to her, even if it caused her physical discomfort or even pain. That is slightly interesting to me. I decide that anything Scarface would let me do to her if I tried to fuck her Alyna would more than likely do with me willingly. As a result I make no small talk with Scarface as she wraps up my clothes.

As I sign the receipt and she gives me my card back along with my bag of clothes, she says, "Hey, I've got a break coming in like five minutes. Do you wanna go get some Starbucks?"

I look at my watch and say, "You know what, I'd actually really like to, but I have to be at my friend's house in fifteen minutes."

She says, "Oh, yeah, that's cool. I just thought maybe, you know. It's cool."

I don't say anything as I exit Banana Republic with my graduation outfit. I get into my car in the parking structure and realize the possibility of this interaction causing Scarface to call me again is not entirely implausible. I hope that she's lost my number as I pull onto Beverly and head back to my apartment, where I jerk off thinking about Scarface eating Alyna out while I fuck her.

chapter forty-four

The Final Final

Alyna hasn't fucked me for the past week, citing the importance of spending every free moment she has studying for her final exams. I accept this excuse only because I have no choice. I do find it strange, though, that she is able to go a week without fucking for finals, or any reason for that matter, based on our previous once-a-day minimum, which has held fast since the third or fourth time we fucked. Despite the fact that she seems to genuinely miss having sex with me, I'm still more alarmed at her ability to omit it from our relationship entirely and feel no significant regret at her decision.

Alyna's last final is at 11:00 A.M. and she's promised to meet me for lunch at my apartment so we can break the dry spell. I've already resigned myself to taking a long lunch despite the consequences at work, which will likely be none. She gets to my apartment at around 1:10 and proceeds to tie me to my bed and fuck me. She alternates between riding my cock, sucking my dick, and jerking me off while she licks my balls, switching her method each time I'm about to cum.

She sits on my dick and plays with her clit as she rocks back and forth. Seeing this makes me blow my load, which she in turn says makes her cum because she can feel my dick throbbing in her cunt.

She gets off my cock and lies down next to me, leaving me tied down. She seems to have genuinely missed fucking me, and based on her performance, most of my concerns about her ability to go without sex are alleviated.

I say, "Untie me."

She says, "Nope."

"What? Untie me."

"Nope. I just took the last test I'll ever take in my life and now I want to spend the rest of your lunch hour doing whatever I want to you. So you're just going to have to lie there and let me do it."

I think back to the first time I saw Alyna on the plane and wondered what she was like in bed. My memory of the event is cut short by Alyna's hand on my cock. She massages it kind of slowly, never letting it get fully hard.

I say, "What're you doing?"

She says, "Whatever I want."

She takes the hand that's not on my dick and starts playing with her clit, then says, "I want to see who I can make cum first."

It's me. I shoot a load all over her hand and all over myself about two minutes after she really gets into giving me a bona fide hand job.

She cums roughly a minute later and then says, "That was pretty fun. I want you to do that to me sometime."

I say, "How about right now?"

She says, "Nope. You don't get to do anything but cum for the next"—she looks at the clock—"thirty minutes."

I say, "I'm taking a long lunch."

"What does that mean?"

"It means I probably have more like an hour."

"Oooh. Then you're definitely not getting untied."

She gets up to get a towel, then comes back and cleans all of the cum off my dick and out of my pubic hair. Then we lie there together for a while.

I say, "What if you fall asleep?"

She says, "Then you're fucked."

She rolls on top of me and looks me in the eyes, then says, "I wouldn't do that to you."

I say, "Thanks."

She takes a second and then says something that makes what was shaping up to quite possibly be the best lunch hour of my life take a nasty turn. She says, "I want to talk to you about something."

She's sitting on top of me and I'm tied down.

She says, "I already know this is going to completely freak you out, but I don't care. . . ."

Not only am I completely freaking out, I'm already trying to rationalize one of three things: (1) how I could have missed the fact that Alyna somehow used to have a dick; (2) how I'm going to cure the herpes that she gave me; or (3) what name would best suit a child I don't want to have.

She says, "What do you think about marriage?"

"What?"

"I know on our first date we both said we thought it was stupid and all of that, and I'm not saying right now. I'm not even saying in the next five years, but what do you think about it in the far, far future?"

I can't believe this is happening to me. I keep waiting for her to tell me that she's just kidding, but it never comes. I'm almost hoping she'll tell me she once had a dick, but she just keeps saying, "Come on, what do you think?"

And as I force myself to actually think about it, I'm surprised to find that the idea of marrying Alyna—as she said, in the far, far future—does not make me want to smash myself in the nuts with a sledgehammer.

I say, "I don't know, why are you asking me this?"

She says, "I don't know. I'm sure it's just because I'm graduating and I don't really know what I want to do with my life and I've just been thinking about a lot of things lately, mainly things that have to do with where my life goes next."

I try to get out of my bonds, but I get nowhere.

I say, "I thought you said in the far future."

"Yeah, I did. I mean, I'm just thinking about what kind of life I could have five or ten years down the road, and I'm not saying this is definitely something I want, but thinking about a life with you doesn't scare me."

I try to imagine being married to Alyna and it doesn't scare me either. It doesn't excite me, but it gives rise to no ill feelings, which is far more than I could have said for a life of being married to Casey. I also realize that this is in no way an admission to myself that I want to marry Alyna.

She says, "I don't want this to turn into some big thing. It's just something I've been thinking about lately and I wanted you to know. I don't want to get married right now, and I don't even really know if I ever do. But the idea of it doesn't sound as bad as it used to. That's all."

I say, "Okay."

She says, "Okay? Are you really okay with this?"

"Yeah." Her terms were vague enough to make me think this might actually be true.

"It doesn't make you want to break up with me?"

She shifts her weight on me and I can feel her wet pussy brush my cock.

"No." This is without a doubt true. Despite her recent slip into a territory I had hoped never to visit again with a girl, she's still hands down the best girlfriend I've ever had.

"Do you still love me?"

Her wet pussy kind of settles right on my cock.

"Yeah."

"Good. I'm glad we talked about this."

She sits back a little and slides her pussy lips along my cock, which is now hard again.

"Me too."

She kisses me and reaches back behind her ass to line my dick up with her cunt. She says, "My mom might bring this up when you meet her," then sits back, and my dick slides into her as she fucks me for the next forty-five minutes.

chapter forty-five

Graduation Day

Alyna stayed at her apartment last night with the excuse that she didn't want to be worn out for her big day. So I jerked off twice before falling asleep and realized that since Alyna and I started dating, the number of times I jerk off in any given week has dropped significantly. Barring the week of her final exams, I estimate my rate of jerking off while dating her to be once or twice a week, usually only to get to sleep if Alyna and I aren't together on a given night. I realize I have never snuck away as Alyna slept to jerk off. The feeling of accomplishment and forward progress I get from this realization makes me eager to see her.

I take a shower and put on the clothes I bought at Banana Republic. Alyna's graduation is in three hours, but I'm supposed to meet up with her so we can go to breakfast and she can introduce me to her family, who she is picking up at the airport.

When I walk into the diner where I'm supposed to meet them, I see Alyna, her dad, who reminds me in no specific way of Casey's dad; her mom, who is a shorter, fatter, uglier version of Alyna; and her two brothers, neither of whom has a wife or children in tow. They all seem nice enough. And it begins.

The brothers give me a few words of caution about dating their sister and let me know not to treat her badly. The mom tells the brothers to back off and the dad keeps asking me what it is I do, even though I've told him multiple times that I don't really do anything important or interesting.

All in all it seems to be going fine and I'm feeling very close to dodging the bullet of a conversation I don't want to have with my girlfriend's parents until Alyna's mom says, "So you guys have been dating for a pretty long time."

And the bullet hits me right between the fucking eyes.

Nobody says anything. Nobody wants her mom to say anything else.

She says, "Now that Alyna's graduating, what do you guys think you'll do?"

I don't know exactly who this question is directed to, but I don't answer. I just take a bite of toast and hope that Alyna will field the question, which she does.

She says, "Mom, I don't know."

Her mom says, "I mean, your father and I got married the week after we graduated from high school, and look at us now."

I can tell Alyna's dad wants to make some kind of joke but he holds it in. I wonder how many weeks after they were married he learned to do that.

Her mom keeps going. "Alyna, you're going to stay out here, right?"

She says, "Yes, Mom. We've already had this conversation."

Her mom says, "Well, if you two love each other, you should at least be living together just to test it out if you don't want to get married right away."

I think about faking a stroke or a seizure so I don't have to listen to her mom anymore, but I don't. Instead I just sit there and let her mom go on and on about how good marriage is. I wonder what her mom would think if she knew I've had my dick in her daughter's ass. I wonder if she's ever taken it up the ass from Alyna's dad.

As she continues to extol the virtues of marriage, an uneasy suspicion works its way through me. It seems more than likely to me that the conversation Alyna had with me about marriage when she had me tied up naked to my bed with my dick in her hand was the direct result of some previous conversation she had with her mother.

I take a sip of my water, which by this point is just ice cubes, to quell the boiling heat in my intestines. I honestly don't know what her mom says for the next ten minutes. All I can think about is that if Alyna and I were to have a daughter, someday Alyna would be telling all the same shit to some poor son of a bitch who just wants to fuck our daughter.

Alyna's parents pay for breakfast and the last thing I remember her mom saying is, "You guys seem like you're practically married now," before we all get in our cars and drive to Alyna's graduation.

I have the amazing privilege of sitting next to her mom during the ceremony.

Laura Ziskin gives the commencement address. I wonder how many cocks she's sucked. I try to remember who spoke at my own graduation but can't. Then the dean comes out and starts handing out diplomas.

As the students start to walk across the stage, Alyna's mom says, "Oh my gosh, doesn't she just look so good in her little cap and gown?"

I look at the stage, where her mom indicates Alyna's sitting, but I can't make her out. She looks the same as all the other twenty-one-year-old girls sitting in their bookstore-rented caps and gowns graduating with degrees in film studies so they can say they went to college before they locked some poor asshole into marriage and kids.

I look out in the crowd of family members and see if I can tell which of the guys are watching their girlfriends graduate knowing their lives will be over as soon as she crosses that stage.

They call her name, "Alyna Janson." She stands up, walks over to the dean, looks out in the crowd, gives her mom a big smile and wave that's caught on at least a dozen pictures snapped by every member of her family, shakes the dean's hand, takes her diploma, and walks back to her seat, where she's once again indistinguishable from everyone else.

The next student does the same thing. And the student after that does the same thing, too.

I hear Alyna's mom whisper to her dad, "Do you remember when we graduated college?"

Then her dad whispers back, "We'd already been married four years and David was a month old."

Her mom whispers back, "I just can't believe our baby is done. She's an adult now."

Her dad whispers back, "We raised her good and she'll do the same for her kids. We did good, Mom. We did good."

I am repulsed by Alyna's dad calling his wife "Mom," and wonder if I had children with Alyna if she'd call me "Dad" or "Father."

That night after I fuck her and pull out to blow my load all over her stomach and tits, I ask her that specific question. Instead of answering it she says, "Have you been thinking about having kids?" with too much enthusiasm to allow me to fall asleep for the rest of the night, despite sneaking into the bathroom twice to jerk off.

some chapter

Diamonds in the Rough

Over the course of my computer-literate life, I've downloaded countless hours of free Internet pornography. On those very rare occasions when I find a clip that is worth repeated viewing, I put it in a folder on my desktop called "Diamonds in the Rough."

As I'm jerking off and downloading movie clips, I find one such clip called cumsisteranna.wmv, in which one girl rides a guy's cock while another licks at his balls, stopping every now and then to take the guy's cock out of the first girl's cunt and suck it before putting it back in and stroking the guy's balls while the first girl keeps fucking him.

I've seen clips like this before and none have seemed as remarkable. I can't quite tell what makes cumsisteranna.wmv stand out. I decide it must have something to do with a subconscious reaction to camera placement or lighting that my untrained eye can't decipher.

I stop jerking off, and as I drag the file into the Diamonds in the Rough folder, I notice that the folder has reached 698MB. The frequency with which I find a clip worthy of being added to the folder is so minuscule that I never would have imagined having enough material to burn an entire disc of porn. I'm almost amazed as I clear my Windows Media Player library and drag all of the files from Diamonds in the Rough into the new library for review.

The first clip that plays is called xxx040.mpg. It features two slightly skinny girls using a double-headed dildo to fuck each other doggie style. The clips that follow are of varied style and subject matter, but for the next forty-five minutes. I watch the porn without jerking off. Instead of the urge to blow a load, the clips strangely conjure nostalgic memories of the girls I was dating when I downloaded them and the computers I downloaded them on.

One specific clip, cumslutsav2.mpg, a fourteen-second clip in which a girl gives a slow, lubricated hand job to a guy whose face you never see, I remember setting to download before I went to fuck my high school girlfriend Katy at one A.M. and coming back two hours later to find it only 76 percent complete on the first Internet-ready computer I ever had.

Another clip, t246.avi, in which a girl deep-throats a dick for thirty seconds without coming up for air, takes me back to Jenna and the time I fucked her in her parents' laundry room while they were in the next room watching *The Omega Code* on the Trinity Broadcasting Network, which in turn reminds me that she is now married to a guy with fucked-up teeth and probably has a kid.

There's a clip of a girl fucking a mechanical dildo doggie style called sybian43.mpg that I jerked off to once while Casey was taking a shower. I blew a load all over myself and had to go into the bathroom she was showering in and pretend to be pissing so I could clean myself off.

I realize the last clip, cumsisteranna.wmv, which I just put in the folder, is the first Diamond in the Rough I've come across since dating Alyna.

As I drag the contents of the entire folder into my Roxio CD burner window and hit the burn button, I wonder how many more Diamonds in the Rough I'll find over the course of our relationship.

As the disk burns I jerk off to an elaborate fantasy involving all the girlfriends I've ever had fucking each other in Jenna's parents' bedroom.

chapter forty-six

Long Story Short

In the week after Alyna's graduation we fucked twice. She gave me one blow job, but finished it by jerking me off. She cited anxiety about her future as the reason for her decreased sex drive.

In the month after Alyna graduated we fucked four times, each time in the missionary position, except once with her on top. She sucked my dick twice, but only after I asked.

In the sixth-month period after her graduation we celebrated our one-year anniversary and fucked forty-seven times, thirty-three of which were initiated by me. I came on her tits six times, each time believing that shooting some of my load "accidentally" on her face might jar her from her increasingly problematic lack of interest in sex.

In the year after Alyna graduated we fucked seventy-four times, the last twelve to fourteen of which were almost like fucking a corpse. During this time, Alyna held various part-time jobs at flower shops and coffeehouses and began taking acting classes at various acting studios. I fucked her in the ass seven times. I jerked off three hundred and thirty-four times, only fantasizing about Alyna twelve times when I actually blew my load.

The relationship has very clearly run its course and this is its final state. I'm surprised this doesn't enrage me more. Instead, Alyna's lack of desire to fuck has given birth to a rapidly growing disinterest in her that strangely hasn't been replaced by interest in anyone or anything else.

It will never be like it was. It will never be better than this.

chapter forty-seven

The End

After an entire morning of lying in my bed watching TV and not fucking, we're sitting outside eating lunch at Swingers in Santa Monica.

She says, "So I think I've figured out what I want to do with this whole acting thing."

I take a bite of scrambled eggs.

"I mean, I like taking acting classes and everything, but I don't think I'm getting anywhere with it. I need to change it up a little."

I take another bite.

"I'm not sure straight acting is what I really want to do anymore. I think I want to try to be like a funny actress, you know, on a sitcom or something. Some of my friends from school are going to take some comedy classes at Improv Olympic and I think I'm going to do it with them, then try to go on some auditions or something. I mean, I live in L.A., right? I might as well give it a shot."

I look over through the big glass wall at a guy sitting across from his girlfriend inside Swingers. She's talking about something as he eats his scrambled eggs and stares into space. I'm pretty sure she's telling him that she wants to be a comedic actress and I'm also pretty sure that they lay in his bed for the entire morning before coming here and I'm also pretty sure she didn't fuck him either.

As Alyna keeps telling me how much fun she thinks comedic acting class will be, I come to a sudden realization that is as horrifying as it is liberating. The uneasy feeling in the pit of my stomach for the past five or six months isn't due to the fact that Alyna seems to have lost her desire to fuck me. It's caused by something else entirely and knowing its source alleviates it completely.

Alyna has slowly become Casey. Aside from her ass, which I'm sure will eventually match Casey's, Alyna has become everything in Casey that made me not want to marry her. Or maybe she was like Casey from the very start but she fucked me so much in the beginning I couldn't see it. Either way, this realization changes something in me.

I look at all the other bitches in Swingers and they all might as well be Casey, or Alyna, or whoever they are.

I take another bite of scrambled eggs knowing that any bitch I ever fuck will ultimately become any other bitch I've ever fucked and they'll all become the fat old bitch eating yogurt in the airport. I look at Alyna and see Casey, Jenna, Katy, and every bitch I've ever fucked or gotten head from or a hand job or even thought about while I jerked off. There is nothing better. There is no fucking escape.

That night we're lying in my bed, both completely naked, watching Conan O'Brien. As Conan interviews Molly Shannon I try to think of all the possible excuses Alyna might use to avoid fucking me tonight. She uses one I did not think of, which is that she's too excited about going to sign up for Improv Olympic classes, and unwittingly sets the following inevitable conversation in motion:

"Alyna?"

She rolls over and says, "Yeah?"

"I was thinking about some things today."

"What things?"

"Just about us and about you."

"What about us and me?"

"Alyna . . ."

"What?"

"Will you marry me?"

Her lack of hesitation as she accepts disgusts me. I wade through an hour of faked joy and hugs and kisses and assurances that we are going to be happy forever. After Alyna calms down, I wait for her to fall asleep without touching my dick and then go to the bathroom and jerk off.

acknowledgments

Mom, thanks for always encouraging me to write and be creative. I'm sorry the end result of that encouragement is something you will not want to read.

Dad, thanks for teaching me self-discipline and thanks for giving me a good education. I know this isn't the same as playing pro-baseball, but it's still pretty cool.

I love you guys and I hope this book doesn't lose you any friends or anything.

THE NOVELS OF CHAD KULTGEN

MEN, WOMEN & CHILDREN

A Novel

ISBN 978-0-06-165731-3 (paperback)

"*Men, Women & Children* explores all of the things that most Americans don't talk about, and in the course of showing what happens when we don't communicate with each other it deftly exposes how we can be both tender and frightening, moving and bizarre, in one of the most beautiful ways I've seen outside of real life." —Stoya

THE LIE

A Novel

ISBN 978-0-06-165730-6 (paperback)

From a writer whose unsettling, brutally honest, and undeniably riotous take on male inner life has rocked readers everywhere comes a dry and cynical tale of three college students who deserve each other.

THE AVERAGE AMERICAN MALE

A Novel

ISBN 978-0-06-123167-4 (paperback)

"It's so primal, so dangerous, it might be the most ingenious book I've ever read."

—Josh Kilmer-Purcell,
New York Times bestselling author of
I Am Not Myself These Days

Visit www.AuthorTracker.com
for exclusive information on your favorite HarperCollins authors.

Available wherever books are sold, or call 1-800-331-3761 to order.